THE CRYPTID FILES:
LOCH NESS

JEAN FLITCROFT

Little Island

First published 2010
by Little Island
An imprint of New Island
2 Brookside
Dundrum Road
Dublin 14

www.littleisland.ie

The author has asserted her moral rights.

ISBN 978-1-84840-940-8

British Library Cataloguing Data. A CIP catalogue record for this
book is available from the British Library.

Book design by Michelle Anderson
Inside design and illustrations by Sinéad McKenna

Printed by ColourBooks Ltd Ireland

Little Island received financial assistance from
The Arts Council (An Chomhairle Ealaíon), Dublin, Ireland.

10 9 8 7 6 5 4 3 2 1

REFERENCES

In the writing of this book I am indebted to a wide range of books and internet sites. I cannot possibly list them all but the following are a wonderful source of information and a great place to learn more about the Loch Ness Monster.

Binns, Ronald, *The Loch Ness Mystery Solved*, Great Britain, Open Books, 1983

Burton, Maurice, *The Elusive Monster: An Analysis of the Evidence from Loch Ness*, London, Rupert Hart-Davis, 1961

Cameron, A.D., *The Caledonian Canal*, Terence Dalton Limited, 1972

Dinsdale, Tim, *Loch Ness Monster*, London, Routledge & Kegan Paul, 1961

Mackal, Roy P., *The Monsters of Loch Ness*, London, Futura, 1976

Shine, Adrian, *Loch Ness, The Loch Ness and Morar Project*

Shine, Maralyn, *Young Loch Ness Explorers, The Loch Ness and Morar Project*

Whyte, Constance, *More Than a Legend: The Story of the Loch Ness Monster*, London, Hamish Hamilton, 1957

Witchell, Nicholas, *The Loch Ness Story*, Terence Dalton Limited, 1974

www.lochnessproject.org
www.lochness.co.uk
www.lochness.co.uk/fan_club
www.nessie.co.uk
www.lochness.co.uk
www.cryptozoology.com
www.cryptomundo.com

CRYPTID FILES:
H NESS

About the author

Dr Jean Flitcroft lives in Dublin with her husband
She started work as a script writer for medical a
and later became a travel writer when her obse
won out. It was on these journeys around the
started writing books for children.

The Cryptid Files: Loch Ness is the first book
covers the globe in pursuit of the weird and wor
of cryptozoology.

www.jeanflitcroft.com

To my children, Oliver, Myles and Callum,
and to children all over the world.

of a series that
she
derful creatures

Acknowledgments

Sincere thanks goes to my friends and writing buddies, Paula, Gemma, Una and Geoff for all their encouragement and helpful comments over the last few years. To Siobhán Parkinson who has been such an inspiration and whose comments and insights have kept me on the right track. Thanks also to Kate Thompson and Conor Kostick for their professional guidance and advice in general.

My thanks to John Short and his talented art students at DIT for their participation in The Cryptid Files Design Competition and Elaina O'Neill in Little Island for making the whole publishing process seem exciting and yet effortless.

And finally to friends and above all family – my wonderful parents, Mary and Alan; brothers Brian and Graham for years of love and support. My heartfelt thanks to my husband Ian for his absolute belief in me, his great insights and his willingness to discuss characters and plots any time and any place, preferably somewhere foreign. And finally to Callum, Myles and Oliver, our fantastic children who inspire me always.

CRYPTOZOOLOGY

The word *cryptozoology* comes from the Greek word *kryptos*, meaning hidden, and *zoology*, meaning the study of animals. Cryptozoologists study animals which may exist in nature, but whose existence has not yet been accepted by modern science.

The animals cryptozoologists search for are called cryptids. The Loch Ness Monster, 'Nessie', is the most famous cryptid of them all, with thousands of recorded sightings.

PROLOGUE

It was the last day of October. The light was fading fast and dark shadows rippled across the surface. A cold wind had picked up and, in the blink of an eye, Loch Ness had changed from a place of yellow sunshine and charm to metal-grey clouds and bleakness.

No one saw Vanessa Day fall. No one saw the tar-coloured water close over her head. For a moment, she was stunned by the icy cold, then terror gripped her and she thrashed about, kicking and slapping the water. She threw her head back, face to the sky, gulping at the air.

But for how long? Her clothes were already waterlogged and the pull of the water relentless. She grabbed at the upturned boat, but the wood was too slimy to grip. Within a few heartbeats, the cold had worked its way into her muscles and her kicks began to grow feeble. In just a few more, her body sagged and then, limp as a ragdoll, she went under.

As she sank she twisted and turned, a slow and deadly dance. Long strands of her black hair were matted across her pretty face. Well before Vanessa reached the bottom, her mouth was wide open and her eyes shut tight.

CHAPTER 1

It is hard to imagine just how deep Loch Ness is. There is more water in it than all the other lakes in England, Wales and Scotland put together. Enough room to fit every person on this earth three times over. Certainly enough room for a few mysteries.

Vanessa crept across the landing. The chill in the early morning had already made its way through her thin cotton nightdress and she wished she had put a sweatshirt on over it. She hesitated for a moment, listening to the stillness of the sleeping house. When she moved on, the silence was broken only by the sticky patter of her bare feet on the wooden floor. She twisted the ring on her middle finger as she walked, anxious in case her footsteps might wake someone. Maybe not her brothers, they would need an earthquake to rouse them, but her dad was a different matter. He had always been a light sleeper and the big fight last night would not have helped matters.

Once she was inside the guest bedroom and onto the thick carpet, she closed the door in slow motion and leaned against it to look around. She hardly ever came into this room and was surprised now at how pretty it was. It was so uncluttered and ordered compared to her own. Looking up, she saw the trapdoor to the attic. Now, where was that long wooden pole with the hook on the end that she needed to open it? It took a couple of minutes to find it under the bed and then much longer to actually hook it through the metal clasp on the trap. Her hands were cold and she found she was shaking with the effort. She twisted and turned it back and forth until it finally flopped open. Next, she had to hook the bottom step of the ladder and pull down hard. The grinding noise was terrible as the ladder unfolded out of the attic, and Vanessa froze, cursing furiously under her breath. That was it, she'd be caught now.

She waited to hear a door open, footsteps on the landing, but there was only silence. She placed her feet carefully on the cold metal and wobbled up, one step at a time. At the top she stared into the gloom. Please God, let there be a light, she thought, as she searched frantically around the opening. She smiled to herself as her fingers found the switch and a harsh white light filled the dusty space.

Vanessa pulled herself up the last step and sat on the floor of the attic, her legs still dangling down through the opening. Row upon row of neatly stacked boxes filled the room. Her heart sank; they all looked identical. Where on earth would she start?

She stood up, crouching over because of the low beams, and looked closely at the lids of the first few boxes. She was relieved to see that each one had a small white label and she recognised the neat italic writing as her father's hand, Marie's history books. The words were like punches to her stomach. One, two and a left hook. Her heart took off, pounding so fast that she felt as if she might faint. Marie's travel books. Marie's research. Her mother's life packed up in boxes. Hot tears filled her eyes and spilled over. Neat boxes labelled and catalogued and stacked in an attic. Her mum would have hated her stuff like this;

she had loved jumble and chaos and life … life. Vanessa felt the sudden urge to overturn every single one of the boxes. Why hadn't she guessed she would feel like this? Why had she come up? Sitting down heavily on one of the boxes, she put her head in her hands and shut her eyes tightly.

She didn't know how long she sat there, but gradually her tears slowed and she began to feel calmer. It started first as a flutter in the pit of her stomach that spread slowly out as a tingle, travelling through every nerve fibre and right to her very fingertips. It had happened once or twice before in the last couple of years. She could feel her mum's presence. She was there with her in that small, bleak attic. It was then that she knew with certainty that she would find what she was looking for.

5.05

CHAPTER 2

Nessie first became famous about 80 years ago, but the locals told stories of a water beast in Loch Ness long before that. They called it a Kelpie. It was a terrible creature that came out of the waters when it was hungry. After transforming into a most beautiful horse, it would wait for someone to climb on its back and then gallop back into the loch to devour them.

It had all started the previous night when Vanessa's father announced at dinner that they would be going on holiday to Scotland for the Hallowe'en midterm break. The delight that followed was worthy of an around-the-world cruise, and Ronan and Luke high-fived boisterously across the table, knocking over a bottle of milk. It was after the milk clean-up, as they were getting down to the details of dates and flights, that her father let slip the fact that Lee McDonald would be coming as well. Luke and Ronan had taken it in their stride as usual, but Vanessa had not. She shouted and ranted and then, running upstairs to her bedroom, finally cried herself to sleep that night behind a locked door.

Vanessa's dreams were often filled with strange winged creatures and shadowy monsters lurking out of sight. But last night was different. One particular monster appeared to her as clear as if she had drawn it herself and the shock of recognition shot through her body like an electric current. She had woken suddenly out of the dream into pitch black. The glowing light on her bedside clock twinkled the ungodly hour of five past five in the morning. Tangled up in her sheets with her head wedged against the wall, Vanessa's physical self felt tired and miserable, but her brain tingled with excitement.

She threw herself back on her bed and pulled her covers tightly up to her neck to think about it some more. Maybe it wasn't a sign as such, but she knew exactly what she had to do that morning. She would have to find her mother's cryptid files. She felt certain that they were the key to her dreams. But where would they be? She twisted her mother's engagement ring on her finger thoughtfully and mentally examined each room in the house. The attic, of course. Two very long years ago, her father had put her mum's things up there. She suspected that nobody had been up since.

The cold in the attic was really beginning to get to Vanessa. Her teeth were chattering now and she rubbed her upper arms vigorously with her hands. How much longer could she last? After another ten minutes moving boxes and reading labels a small frisson of doubt began to seep in. What if the cryptid files had got lost or had been thrown away? In her growing unease, Vanessa failed to notice a low wooden box in front of her. She tripped and fell heavily, grimacing with the pain as her knees hit the floor beams. So much for being quiet, she thought. She hunkered into a sitting position and then waited, motionless and listening. It was only then that she noticed the blood and the gash on her knee, which was bleeding profusely. Irritated with herself for being so clumsy, she bunched the end of her nightdress into a ball and pressed it to her cut, glaring at the box. Her eyes widened with surprise. Rather than her father's neat handwriting on a label, she saw the big capital letters scrawled across the wooden lid. Even upside down she could read her mother's bold writing: THE CRYPTID FILES. They had found her.

She took a few moments to examine the box before opening the lid. It was old and very battered with rusty hinges and Vanessa couldn't recall seeing it before. What if there was nothing in it or it was just full of old shoes? The disappointment might be too much. She ran her hand slowly over the wood and then finally pushed open the lid. A tiny shrunken head stared up at her and she dropped the lid back down. Opening the lid again, she stared hard at the empty eyes and the puckered skin. It was a human head, she felt sure, but what was it doing in her attic? Slowly something stirred in her memory. Something to do with her grandfather Todd, wasn't it? Picking the head up gingerly, she found that it fitted perfectly into the palm of her small hand. She tried to remember the story of a tribal chief in Papua New Guinea that had given it to him, but the memory danced just out of reach. Instead she heard her mother's voice.

'Life without adventure is no life at all.'

At bedtime when she was small, instead of reading about ballerinas and princesses, her mum had told her stories of wicked Incan gods and strange animals with magical powers. As she grew up, Vanessa was actually proud that her mother never did the things that other mothers did. Even before her illness, she never bothered much about the ordinary stuff – the car pooling, haircuts, coffee mornings, sales of work. Instead her world was full of the extraordinary – myths and cryptids, archaeological artefacts from various digs and, her most prized possession of all, an enormous antique world map, which took up an entire wall of Vanessa's bedroom. It was covered in dots – red ones for places they had already visited, green for ones they had to visit within the next five years, orange for the next ten years and purple for the outside chance ones. They spent many hours poring over it and discussing travel. No wonder Vanessa's end-of-year school reports always referred to her as a determined day dreamer. One had said: 'If Vanessa put as much energy into real life as her imaginary world, she might just scrape by in her exams …'

'Excellent,' her mother had said as she threw the report into the wood-burning stove, 'there's nothing like an imagination to get you through life.'

A door banging downstairs in the house startled Vanessa back into action. Hurriedly, she pushed the shrunken head into the pocket of her nightdress; there was no time to lose. The box was full of coloured folders but she recognised the one she wanted immediately – a red plastic ring-binder with a charcoal picture stuck to the front. It looked so smudged and childish to her now – her first sketch of the most famous cryptid of them all: Nessie, The Loch Ness Monster, the creature of her dreams.

CHAPTER 3

In 1934, a local bye-law was introduced to protect the Loch Ness Monster. If the monster is just a myth, why does it need real laws to protect it?

Back in her bedroom, Vanessa snuggled down under her duvet with her cryptid folder. Maybe she could spend the rest of the day in bed and avoid seeing her father at all. Bed was the best place to be on miserable days.

A bang on the door made her start. Luke or Ronan, she guessed, hardly her father. Either way, they knew better than to open the door without an invitation.

'Vanessa, can I borrow your new tennis racket? I'm

playing doubles this morning and I don't want to show myself up,' Ronan shouted loudly through the closed door.

'Best not to play then, Ronan,' she shouted back unsympathetically.

'Oh come on, Vanessa, you owe me.'

She hesitated. Was he referring to the scene last night? He was far too kind for that. She remembered the look on her dad's face when she had accused him of betraying her mum's memory. She felt guilty for saying it in front of everyone, but she really had meant it. Her upper lip curled in distaste. Imagine wanting to bring Lee McDonald on a family holiday to Scotland! It was bad enough having her come for dinner so often. She remembered now the rush of adrenaline, the outrage that had reached her lips before she could cool her reaction. She felt the anger flare inside her again. How dare he mention her mum in the same breath as Lee McDonald!

'Come on, Vanessa, please?'

'OK, but if you break it or lose it, you're dead.'

She heard him whoop as he sped down the stairs before she changed her mind. Ronan wasn't bad compared to other younger brothers she had met. Of course he missed their mum terribly, but, two years

12

on, both he and Luke seemed to be really well adjusted. And yet two years on, things were getting worse and not better for her, Vanessa thought darkly.

She opened the first few pages of the Loch Ness folder and a thrill shot through her. There was one section on the geography of Loch Ness and two on the scientific arguments – one for and one against. And her favourite section – the sightings. These were stories of little old ladies and children, priests and fishermen. Her mother had downloaded hundreds off the internet. She scanned the dozens of pages. Surely they couldn't all be pranksters or lunatics?

Witness: Sir Graham McDonald and sons Brian and Ben
Date: 7 August 1934 at 5 p.m.
Description: While fishing on the banks of the loch they saw a creature with one hump about 15 feet in length. It remained stationary for about a minute and then moved off at speed.

Witness: Mrs Elizabeth Allen and Mrs Agnes Thomas
Date: 2 October 1946, mid-afternoon
Description: Noticed something in the water as

they drove. When they stopped they saw a single
hump moving slowly but producing a large wake.
It appeared and disappeared a couple of times.

She wondered what Mrs Thomas and Mrs Allen had been doing at the time. Were they in an ancient black car with a picnic basket and a rug on the back seat, their dog, Cricket, pawing at the basket, desperate to get at the roast chicken? Had they almost crashed the car when they saw the humped monster appear in front of them? She imagined them as two frail English ladies of impeccable character with horn-rimmed glasses. Who could believe that this unlikely pair would make it all up?

Witness: Miss Jennifer Grant
Date: 10 August 1986 at 11.30 a.m.
Description: Head and long neck sticking out of the water. It sank slowly as she watched it. Two photos taken but only ripples visible in both.

She could imagine young Jennifer, a university student, on her way to visit her aunt in Inverness. Standing on the bank near Urquhart Castle, paralysed as a snake-like neck rises out of the water.

14

Her reactions so slowed with shock that she misses Nessie in her photo.

Vanessa stopped reading and let the folder fall back onto the bed. Did her mother believe in Nessie or was it just more of her 'weird and wonderfuls', as the boys used to call her stories? What if she had believed? Wouldn't it be incredible to prove her right, especially after all these years of scientists and journalists on the hunt?

'I'd like to be a cryptozoologist when I grow up, Miss.' Vanessa smiled at the thought of saying it to Miss Carter, her pathologically dull headmistress, and wondered what her reaction would be.

'A what?'

Vanessa would have to explain.

'You mean you want to chase imaginary monsters for a living? Childish nonsense. It's time to grow up, Vanessa Day.'

But her own mother, a rational, grown-up academic with a doctorate from Oxford, had done just that.

Vanessa pulled out her shrunken head from her nightdress pocket and stared intently at the wizened face and tiny beady black holes for eyes. It was such an ugly little face and yet so compelling. As she stared at the mouth, her mind played tricks and she saw it move ever so slightly. She knew it wasn't the tiny head that whispered, but she heard it all the same.

Go and find what you are looking for. The words rolled around in her mind and then took root. Perhaps a holiday in Scotland might not be such a bad idea after all.

CHAPTER 4

In Scots Gaelic, the monster was known as Niseag, which got shortened to Nessie. Then, in 1975, Nessie was given the proper scientific name of Nessiteras rhombopteryx *by the president of the World Wildlife Fund at the time, Sir Peter Scott.*

During the weeks after the big row, there was no further mention of the family holiday. The days rolled by and Vanessa noticed that Lee was much less in evidence than before. She saw her father most evenings, if only briefly, before bed. He was working far too hard, according to Mrs Gannon, who came in the afternoons to prepare dinner and recreate some semblance of normal family life.

In the days leading up to her tests before the mid-term break, Vanessa tried to focus on revising, but trade and industry graphs and irregular French verbs were of little interest compared to the stories of Nessie.

On the Thursday of that week, when Vanessa came down to breakfast, she found a brand new Dorling Kindersley guide book to Scotland on the kitchen table.

'Did Dad leave this book out, Luke?' Vanessa eyed it suspiciously.

'Don't know,' Luke grunted as he spooned mounds of Rice Krispies into his mouth hungrily. 'He's gone to work,' he added, as if that explained it.

'Are we going to Scotland after all?' Ronan asked innocently.

'Dad didn't mention it again,' Luke offered without looking up from his bowl.

Vanessa's mouth went dry. Suddenly she didn't feel like breakfast. Looking at Luke and Ronan busily feeding themselves, she realised that she might have cheated them out of a much-needed holiday, and lost her chance to visit Loch Ness.

'Sorry,' she mumbled, and, when no one acknow-ledged it, she went on: 'You know I'd love to go to

Scotland, but I'm not going with her.' Her voice rose defensively.

'She's not that bad, Vanessa,' Ronan said, looking directly at her.

'Isn't she?'

'OK, she's not Mum, but who can be? You should at least be fair,' Luke added. 'She's not the devil either.'

Vanessa felt the hairs on the back of her neck stand up, and her temper flare, but she managed to keep her mouth shut this time. Fair, Luke had said. Fair? Why the hell should she be fair? Fair had absolutely nothing to do with it.

CHAPTER 5

Some sightings may be honest mistakes. The wind blowing across the surface, a large seal or a floating log might play tricks on someone's eye. What is hard to explain is where lots of people, sometimes from several locations on the loch, witness the monster at the same time.

Vanessa Day's house was a large detached red-brick at the end of a leafy green cul-de-sac. Her bedroom looked out over the front garden, and she could see the apple and pear trees in the centre of the lawn and the stone path that meandered through them. But her favourite tree was in the back garden – a huge lime tree, which stood over 100 feet tall and had views into the neighbours' gardens. For years now, it had been her and her best friend Grace's den.

Looking down at the car in the drive, she could see Luke putting his bag into the boot. As he walked back to the house, he looked up and signalled to her, pointing at his watch. She waved back, but instead of running downstairs, she turned on her computer. Logging into her email account she wrote:

> Hi Gracie. Guess what? I was right after all!!!! You know I told you about the book on Scotland appearing on the table? Well, last night, tickets for the four of us magically appeared on the mantelpiece. We are flying to Inverness first (LOCH NESS!!!!) and then getting the train to Edinburgh. Imagine a whole week of holiday, but best of all SHE's never been mentioned again! My freak out must have worked!!

'For God's sake Vanessa, will you hurry up?' her dad shouted up impatiently. Vanessa pressed the Send button, closed down the computer, shoved her book and her fleece into her bag and ran down the stairs out to the car as fast as she could.

'Well, let's hit the road, Alan.'

'Your belt please, Vanessa,' her father answered sharply.

She knew he disliked it when she called him by his first name. Tough, he did lots of stuff that she didn't like.

'Ignore her, Dad. Come on, let's go,' Ronan piped up as he punched Vanessa lightly on the arm. He didn't want another fight starting.

The lines of cars stretched as far as the eye could see. The M50 could be slow, but today it seemed to be at a full stop. Vanessa looked at her watch. Their flight was at half three and it was already one o'clock. Her father hated being late for anything and she could feel his stress. The muscles in the back of his neck were taut and she was suddenly aware of the amount of grey in his thick black hair. She hadn't noticed before and was quite unprepared for the wave of sadness that ran through her. Pressing her forehead against the cool of the window, she stared through the blur of her tears. She cried over the silliest of things these days.

The plane was more crowded than she had expected and when she found her row, she moved quickly into the window seat. The boys would want to sit together anyway.

How she envied them their closeness sometimes! They were so alike despite the five-year age difference. 'The twins' her mother used to call them. She looked across the aisle at them, their heads bent together. What did they talk about? Luke was getting a pack of cards out of his bag. Typical! No doubt they would play cards for the entire flight. Luke had recently moved on from wanting to be in the army and was now considering a career as a professional poker player.

Her father put his bag in the overhead locker and sat down beside her with his book. Vanessa flipped open the red folder on her knee and began to read:

Loch Ness is at the northern end of the Great Glen fault line that cuts across the Highlands of Scotland. 24 miles long and 1 mile wide, it is up to 1,000 feet deep at certain points. It holds more water than all the lakes and reservoirs in England and Wales together and it could hold all the people in the world three times over.

'My God, I had no idea it was that deep; no wonder they can't find her!' Her father had been reading the page over her shoulder. Vanessa looked straight at him to see if he was just teasing her, but his face was quite serious.

'I know, it's amazing, isn't it? People can't dive down that deep, so how can they possibly know she doesn't live at the bottom?'

'Well . . .' her father paused, 'I suppose if she is a plesiosaurus or something dinosaur- or mammal-like then she has to breathe air and she would have to come to the surface all the time.'

'Yes, I know, but some scientists believe that there are caves and tunnels and she could come up for air in there. Look.'

She turned to a section marked 'geology' and read out loud:

During a coastguard exercise, a large cavern was discovered in Loch Ness at a depth of 800ft near Urquhart Bay. Locals now call it Edward's Deep after the man who found it. This may be the entrance to a whole network of caves, the access point into Nessie's home and the reason she can stay hidden during searches.

'Urquhart Bay,' Vanessa murmured to herself, 'where are we staying, Dad?'

'At Fort Augustus. I think it's at the south end of Loch Ness.'

'Fort Augustus! Oh, Dad, some of the most important sightings have happened there. You just have to read this.' She pointed to a picture of a man, his right hand raised and his index finger pointing at something. 'That's Father Gregory, a monk from Fort Augustus Abbey.'

Her father read on:

On October 14 1971, Father Gregory Brusey of the Benedictine Abbey in Fort Augustus and a friend, Roger Pugh, saw 'a terrific commotion in the waters of the bay ... we saw quite distinctly the neck of the beast standing out of the water to ... a height of about 10 feet. It swam towards us at a slight angle, and after about 20 seconds slowly disappeared, the neck immersing at a slight angle. We were at a distance of about 300 yards ...'

'Would a monk who is devoting his life to God really make up such a story?' Vanessa was genuinely puzzled.

'Well, I should hope not. But what's the evidence

on the other side? The "Nessie doesn't exist" argument?' Her dad, always the lawyer, dug her gently in the ribs.

'Well, there's not as much as you might think. There were certainly some fake photographs done, the most famous one by an English doctor that's called the surgeon's photo. But one fake photograph doesn't take away from all the other sightings. You know there are thousands of eyewitness accounts: priests, politicians, film crews, lords and ladies, children even. I don't believe they all lied.'

She looked up at him, all excitement, and, suddenly, her dad leaned over and, pushing her hair back off her forehead, kissed her tenderly. Vanessa blinked in surprise and patted his arm companionably. He rested his head back against the seat rest and closed his eyes.

Vanessa took a quick sideways look at his face and felt a sharp pang of guilt. He looked very sad when his face was resting, she thought, sad and old. She knew that she made his life difficult sometimes, particularly in the past few weeks. She would make it up to him now that they were on their own. It would be wonderful to have a normal family holiday together.

The short flight was over far too quickly for

Vanessa. She had only got about a third of the way through her file. The boys had played cards all the way.

'Look, we're coming in to land,' Ronan said loudly.

Luke caught Vanessa's eye. 'I've cleaned Ronan out again. Fancy trying to win back his money?'

'How much?' Vanessa was very good at poker and often beat Luke.

'Thirty.'

'Sterling? You thief, you know he doesn't have much money.'

'You could try and win it back for him this evening.'

'OK, but be prepared to lose every cent you've brought.' Vanessa tried to look stern, but she couldn't resist smiling at him. She had a good feeling about this trip.

Vanessa felt the sudden jolt as the plane landed and ran along the runway. The plane came to a halt, and she pressed her head to the plastic covering the window and felt the excitement rise up in her. She could see a large blue sign over a modest and rather dull building: 'Welcome to Inverness'.

CHAPTER 6

There are four freshwater lochs in the Great Glen: Loch Dochfur, Loch Ness, Loch Oich and Loch Lochy. These lochs are connected to the sea by a 100 kilometre long waterway called the Caledonian Canal and, in parts, by the River Ness. There are 29 locks and 10 bridges along the length of the canal.

While they all waited at the car rental desk, Vanessa spotted a bookshop at the end of the arrivals hall.

'I'll get the road-maps, Dad, if you give me some money.' Vanessa wanted to get a good ordnance survey map of Loch Ness for herself.

He pulled out his wallet and handed her a fifty-pound note.

'I'll need lots of change from that.' He grinned. 'Oh, and get me a map of the Isle of Skye. I think it's only a couple of hours' drive. I've always wanted to visit.'

She found the rack with tourist books and maps. Beside it, the shelves were filled with bright, kelly- green dinosaurs with red tartan berets. Nessie was emblazoned across their chests. She turned her back on them, disdainfully. How tacky! What a cheap way to represent the most famous cryptid in the entire world!

She opened nearly every map on display, examining each one carefully before folding them back, much to the displeasure of the shop assistant.

'Can I help you at all?' she asked at last.

Oblivious to the implied criticism, Vanessa replied cheerfully, 'Oh, no thanks. I just want to make sure I get the right one.'

In the end, Luke was sent in to get her. He tried to dissuade her from buying four maps. But Vanessa was adamant. She needed a general road-map of the Highland area, a detailed map of the Isle of Skye for her father, a map showing the different lochs along the Great Glen, including Loch Ness, and the best one of all – a detailed map of Loch Ness itself. It showed the gradients of the loch sides, the water depth and also lots of detail about the canal locks at the north and south ends.

The rental car was a Ford Ka, with an engine that sounded like a small tractor.

'Whoever wants to navigate sits in the front. I'll have to put my seat right back, so the back seat is going to be pretty tight, sorry.'

Their father fiddled with his seat position. His long legs would sometimes go into cramp if he sat too close. They should have rented something bigger, Vanessa thought. Her father looked ridiculous in the front seat, oversized and awkward.

'I'll navigate,' Ronan said eagerly.

'I'll sit behind you, Dad,' Vanessa offered helpfully.

In truth, Vanessa just wanted time to study the Loch Ness map quietly. Normally, Vanessa or her mother would have done the map reading. Vanessa had a great sense of direction and had the distinct advantage of being the only person in the family able to refold maps properly. Ronan, on the other hand, was a disaster. He would open the map out fully so that it covered the gear stick and he almost always ended up tearing the map.

Luke had his iPod headphones firmly fixed in his ears, lost to all the negotiations. Without a word, he opened the back door and slid in beside Vanessa. Vanessa considered her older brother. He had got tall recently. He was sprawled across the back seat, his gangly legs and bony elbows taking up most of the space.

'Move over, freak.'

'Keep it nice, Vanessa,' her father said mildly, watching them in the rear-view mirror.

Immediately outside the airport, they found the road south to Inverness. It was a beautiful afternoon. Sunlight filtered through the tall silver birch forests and the sky was a true blue. It was pure magic for Vanessa and her eyes kept wandering from the map to the scenery.

'Look. Just up ahead, you see that funny turret and the roof of the castle? That's Castle Stuart,' Ronan said proudly. 'It's on my map.'

They slowed as they passed the gates and read the plaque: 'Accommodation only by prior arrangement'.

'Imagine staying there. Maybe sometime we could do that, Dad?'

'Perhaps on another trip,' Alan replied non-committally.

'Where are we staying in Fort Augustus? Is it a guest house?' Vanessa asked.

'No, a cottage. It's right on the banks of Loch Ness. Ronan, is there a right-hand turn coming up shortly?'

Vanessa went back to her maps.

It wasn't long before she got her first glimpse of Loch Ness. It was grander and more impressive than any picture she had seen. Backed by huge pine-covered mountains and lined at the water's edge by ancient silver birches, everything glistened in the sunlight.

'Turn left, turn left,' she shouted suddenly from the back seat. She had spotted a sign half covered with a shrub for the Dochgarrach Locks.

'What is it Vanessa?'

'Lock Dochgarrach, can we see it please? It's the first of the lock-gates on the northern end of Loch Ness.'

'You mean L-O-C-H,' Ronan corrected her.

'No, I mean L-O-C-K,' said Vanessa. 'A loch is a lake. But this is a lock, like we have on the canal at home. Lock-gates, you can call them. Lock Dochgarrach is a lock, Loch Ness is a loch.'

'Boring, boring,' droned Ronan, 'I want to get to the cottage. I'm starving.'

'There will be lots of time to explore the locks, I promise. We have three days here.' Her father sounded firm, his 'no room for argument' sort of voice, and Vanessa let it go. She was dying to see the cottage too.

CHAPTER 7

A large number of salmon migrate through Loch Ness to their breeding ground. The eels in Loch Ness travel even farther – all the way to the Sargasso Sea. The loch is no stranger to visitors.

About half an hour later, they came to the small village of Drumnadrochit and the site of the official Loch Ness visitors' centre. Her father slowed the car, but didn't stop.

'We'll do that too,' he offered, before Vanessa could ask. She could see a sea of green Nessie teddies hanging outside the shop. This time, they held red bagpipes. Above them a large billboard carried an advert for the Express Loch Ness Monster Boat. 3D sonar on board, it said, followed by a huge exclamation mark. Vanessa hoped her father wouldn't suggest that – she'd hate it. She'd much prefer to take a small quiet fishing boat out on the loch and get the real atmosphere that way.

As they approached the village of Fort Augustus, Vanessa's spirits soared. One, two, three, four, five. Five locks and a swing bridge! And this was where they were staying.

'Look at those lock-gates!'

'Why such interest in lock-gates all of a sudden?' Alan sounded surprised.

'Well …' Vanessa hesitated. She had never shared her theory with anyone about how Nessie had got into Loch Ness. 'Well, Mum and I thought that the locks might have something to do with it.'

'With what?' Ronan piped up.

'The explanation for how Nessie got here. You see, a very long time ago, the Great Glen fault line ran from the east coast of Scotland all the way across to the west. This meant that the lochs, including Loch Ness, were actually linked to the sea. One of the main theories is that when that connection closed off, about ten thousand years ago, Nessie became trapped in Loch Ness.' She stopped. They wouldn't be interested.

'And?' Luke prompted her. Vanessa was surprised. She had thought that Luke was listening to his music. Now, she noticed that one of the ear pieces was out and lying on his shoulder.

'Well, there has always been the problem that in order for a Nessie species to survive and evolve over ten thousand years, there would need to be quite a big number of Nessies breeding and a lot of fish for them to eat. Whereas I think, well we thought …'

'Go on.' Her father glanced in the mirror, his face eager.

'Well, it's possible that Nessie did come from the sea, but not ten thousand years ago. I think she's a deep-sea mammal that got trapped by following salmon migrating through the Caledonian Canal into Loch Ness.'

'Hang on. I thought you said that the access to the sea had been closed off ten thousand years ago,' Luke pointed out.

'Well, yes, it was, but it was opened up again when they built the Caledonian Canal linking Loch Ness to the sea through a series of lock-gates. There are twenty-nine of them in total, and that means fishing boats can cut across Scotland from the Irish Sea to the Atlantic without going around the top. And – this is what clinches it – the locks and the canal were finished in 1822, which just happens to be around the same time people started to see a monster in the loch!'

Luke got it. 'So, you mean there isn't a whole bunch of them, breeding away and evolving? There's just this one lonely monster who got trapped?'

'Exactly. And that's why I'm interested in the locks,' she added. 'You see?'

'Not a bad theory, even for you, Vanessa,' Luke said mildly.

Vanessa dug him in the ribs with her elbow, without bothering to look at him. She enjoyed the gasp of pain elicited.

'We're here.' Alan slowed the car in front of a pair of ancient wrought-iron gates.

He edged the car through the narrow opening and into a steep drive that was lined by trees. Vanessa could see the stone cottage at the end. It was implausibly beautiful, the most beautiful house she had ever seen. She knew exactly how Hansel and Gretel had felt stumbling upon the gingerbread house. Three small windows nestled in the roof looking over the loch. A climber with white flowers bushed over the door arch and there was even a small white cat waiting by the front door. Vanessa looked down the slope of the garden to the water's edge where a wooden bench perched on the edge of the loch. She was entranced.

'Catch, Vanessa,' Ronan shouted playfully as he turfed her bag out of the boot onto the driveway. The cat didn't move as they approached the door and merely stared back at them with the occasional flick of her ear. They rang the bell and waited. It opened slowly to reveal a small woman with grey hair and twinkling eyes. It was too much. Vanessa felt as if she had been unwittingly trapped in a fairy tale.

'Welcome, welcome, come in, come in. You must be starving after that long journey. I've scones and tea made.'

Her soft Scottish accent and kind words drew them in and they all but fell through the door in a heap.

CHAPTER 8

Loch Ness researcher, Adrian Shine, has said, 'If monsters exist, then science, a mainstay of our conventional wisdom, has ignored the most exciting wildlife mystery in the British Isles. If there are none, then over a thousand people including doctors, clergymen, MPs, civil dignitaries, not to mention a saint, may have lied; unthinkable. Alternatively, they were sincerely and unshakably mistaken; even more worrying!'

The hall was narrow and they all stood in a clump in the middle of it, not sure how to proceed.

'Oh, in to the left, children. I've set a fire for you.'

It wasn't a cold afternoon, but the flames flickering

in the grate were a welcome sight. The room smelled of something familiar and when Vanessa looked around, the room she saw pots brimming with lavender. She didn't remember ever having seen lavender plants indoors, but she did remember the fragrance well because her mother used to spray it on her pillow when she couldn't sleep. She used to think that it was like a magic potion because it worked on her so quickly.

Vanessa left her bag against the wall and sat down in one of the armchairs in front of the fire, curling her long legs under her like a cat. She liked it here already.

'Cream and jam for everybody?'

'I'll help you,' Vanessa offered spontaneously, standing up again from her chair.

Her father smiled at her, pleased to see that she was making an effort.

'Well, that would be kind, thank you, dear.'

The tea ceremony took about fifteen minutes and while the boys ate heartily and chatted on, Vanessa found herself getting sleepier. Perhaps it was the effect of the lavender. She opened her eyes with an effort, to find the elderly woman gazing directly at her.

'Come on, Vanessa. I'll show you your room and

maybe you could have a short rest before supper.'

Vanessa's legs felt like lead as she mounted the stairs. Her room was one of the rooms to the front with the window looking over the loch.

'It's gorgeous, thank you. And it looks out over the water.'

'Maybe you'd like to go out on the loch tomorrow morning?' The old lady gazed out of the window. 'It's always most beautiful first thing,' she added. Before Vanessa could answer, she continued on, 'We'll ask Lee when she comes back. She's out on the loch at the moment. She always takes the boat out for an hour or two when she arrives home, especially if she's been away for a while.'

CHAPTER 9

23 April 1960 was a day that changed Tim Dinsdale's life. He filmed an object in Loch Ness moving at about 10 mph with his cine camera. An aeronautical engineer, Tim gave up his job and devoted the next twenty years to investigating the Loch Ness Monster. In 1966, the Royal Air Force studied the film and came to the conclusion that it was a living object rather than a vessel or submarine.

Vanessa waited until the door closed before she lay down on the bed and buried her face in the pillow. She sobbed quietly, her head and heart were aching and she felt sick to her stomach with the disappointment.

How could he do this to her? He hadn't mentioned Lee McDonald again after their argument. How sneaky to have her show up here rather than at the airport! No doubt everybody else knew all about it. Luke or Ronan might have warned her.

She dug her hand into the pocket of her jacket and pulled out her shrunken head. Holding it close to her face calmed her, but with it came an overwhelming fatigue. Crawling under the covers and pulling them up over her head, Vanessa closed her eyes and begged her mother to help her out of this one.

She ignored the light tap on the door and didn't lift her head when she heard someone come quietly into the room and across to the bed. She didn't want to talk to anyone. She felt the hand rest lightly on the back of her head, and then gently stroke her hair. She pulled at the bed cover so that she could see out. Peeking through the fringe of lashes she saw the tweed skirt of the old woman. Was she Lee's mother? Neither of them spoke, and Vanessa shut her eyes again, letting the gentle strokes soothe her, just like her own mother had.

When Vanessa woke, the room was in darkness. The sleep had refreshed her and she felt back in fighting spirits. Turning on the bedside lamp, she saw that there was a small basin in the corner of the room. The water from the tap felt ice cold as she patted it onto her face. Feeling much more alert, she looked around for her bag. She wanted to brush her teeth as well. Damn, it was downstairs in the sitting room.

The fire was still blazing, but the room was empty, except for the white cat curled up on the chair closest to the fire. Stroking its back distractedly, Vanessa looked out of the window into the garden. It was getting dark but she could make out two figures on the bench at the end of the garden. Alan and Lee were sitting one at each end. Not close at all. Was that for her benefit, she wondered?

She could hear noise coming from another room down the hall. Ronan's voice rose over the rest.

'Can I have a go at picking one up?'

Vanessa followed the sound, turning in to the doorway of a large kitchen which had a long oak table in the centre. She counted quickly: it was set for nine people. Ronan and Luke were standing either side of the old woman facing the Aga cooker. On the floor stood a huge black bucket filled with crabs.

'Maggie. Please. I won't let them nip me. Just show me how to do it again.'

Maggie, indeed! All very cosy.

Vanessa hesitated at the door.

'Vanessa, come and help us. I need someone who can chop the garlic finely for the garlic butter sauce. Someone I could trust with an extremely sharp knife.'

Holding the tip, Maggie held out the handle of the knife in Vanessa's direction. Vanessa could see it was a gesture of trust and that she was being asked to do the same. Trust me, Maggie's eyes said. They were kind and warm, and Vanessa went with her instincts, joining her by the stove. Did she trust herself with the knife? Vanessa thought wryly.

'I've just been telling the boys to call me Maggie, Margaret is so formal. I never liked the name anyway.'

Vanessa smiled despite herself. There was nothing at all formal about this small, chatty woman.

Twenty minutes later, the salad and bread on the table, the door bell rang.

'Oh, that will be the Mackays.' Maggie moved slowly to the hall to answer the door. Vanessa glared viciously at the boys, waiting for her moment.

'Vanessa, will you get Lee and Alan for me? We must eat the crab fresh from the cooking pot, there's no other way. That door takes you to the garden, dear. Gently now.'

Vanessa was unsure whether Maggie said it because the back door was sticking as she tried to yank it open or because she knew Vanessa was in a right temper.

She followed the stone pathway as it meandered down to the water front. Halfway down, she stopped. What would she say?

Before she could think of anything Alan turned around. 'Did you have a good rest, Vanessa?'

The question, delivered in such an easy tone, made her rear up. She all but spat the answer back at him.

'The dinner's ready when you are.'

She stood silently, glaring at him and ignoring Lee.

They rose as one and they made their way up the garden. As they approached, Vanessa made her move, willing herself not to cry.

'Could I talk to you before you go in?'

Her father, evidently hoping that this meant a truce, stopped beside her. He put his hand lightly on her shoulder and gave her an encouraging smile, while Lee took her cue and continued up the garden.

She waited until the kitchen door closed and then shrugged his hand off.

'How could you do this to me?' When he didn't answer straight away, she rushed on. 'You could have told me at some point on the way that she was coming, even worse, that we were staying in her house. I hate you, I'll never forgive you for this. You know what I think of her!' Her voice was shrill and she shouted the last sentence.

'Come down by the water's edge and we'll talk, Vanessa.' She didn't move, but he walked on himself. When she finally joined him, he said quietly, 'I didn't tell you because I knew you'd make a scene and refuse to come.'

'Damn right,' she said bitterly.

'Which would be a terrible pity, because I know how much Loch Ness means to you and that staying right on the loch would be really special.'

'Well if you knew that, why do it this way? Why couldn't we come on our own and stay in a B&B like we normally do?' A lump formed in her throat suddenly and she swallowed hard to stop the tears coming.

'Because Lee is a good friend and she asked us to come and stay with Maggie.'

'No. She asked *you* to come and stay with Maggie.'

'No, she asked us all actually.'

'Well, what a lovely family outing, complete with Lee's mother rather than our own!' Vanessa said it in the most sarcastic tone she could manage.

'We are here as a family, Vanessa,' her father said calmly, 'and by the way, Maggie is Lee's aunt.'

Vanessa stared at him, amazed to find that she felt relieved. Why did an aunt not sound as bad to her?

'I suppose Luke and Ronan knew all about Maggie.'

'No, I didn't say anything to them either.'

'You're mean and dishonest and you should be ashamed of yourself,' she whispered bitterly. 'How could you have forgotten Mum so quickly?'

'Quickly?' Her father said faintly. 'Oh, Vanessa, I'll never forget; how could I? She was my wife, my best friend in the whole world, but I can't help that she died. It's been the longest, loneliest time of my life.'

'Well, it's not exactly been a picnic for me either,' Vanessa said brutally, and she turned on her heels and stomped up the path to the house.

CHAPTER 10

On 15 June 1965, Detective Sergeant Cameron was fishing on the shores of Loch Ness. He saw a whale-like object between 20 and 30 feet long moving against the current. Other people witnessed the same event; it lasted nearly 40 minutes and is one of the longest incidences on record.

The party was well under way when Vanessa returned to the kitchen. Nobody noticed her coming in from the garden. Some of the guests were gathered around the Aga discussing how best to cook crabs. Lee was sitting at the table laughing with two implausibly old men. One had wrinkles all over the top of his bald head ending in folds of skin at the back of his neck, while the other had a head of white hair and a beard that would have put St Nicholas to shame.

There was a whiff of madness in the air, she thought; this was no average gathering. Maybe she could slip away up to her bedroom with her book and say she wasn't feeling well. She certainly felt nauseated at the thought of spending the evening with Lee's friends and family.

Before she could take another step, the sound of scraping on the floor under the kitchen table was followed by a blur of red hair which flew through the air and landed hard against her chest. Vanessa stumbled backwards, banging against the kitchen door amidst the cries of the rest of the party, who had suddenly noticed her. Mayhem ensued. Barks, shouts, laughter. Rolling onto her side to stop the beast from licking her face, Vanessa lay in a foetal position with her hands covering her face until someone dragged it off. She liked dogs, but not that much.

'Stop that, Daisy, behave yourself,' a man with a thick Scottish accent shouted, as he dragged the dog off her by the collar.

Vanessa sat up as quickly as she could, noticing that it was the bald one who'd spoken.

'Well, I must say, she likes you.' He smiled down at her, before offering her a hand up.

'Stupid dog should be put down,' the one with all the hair grumbled crankily.

'No, no, she's fine, honestly,' Vanessa said, suddenly afraid that he really meant it.

'She's an Irish red setter. We brought her to dinner because we thought you might like to meet a fellow countrywoman,' the bald one explained.

'A witch's dog if you ask me,' the hairy one grumbled. 'Should be douked like the witches themselves.'

'Hush now, you'll scare the child with that kind of talk.'

Vanessa's face lit up.

'What's douking then?' she asked the hairy one.

He paused, taking the measure of Vanessa before he explained.

'In the old days, if a woman was accused of being a witch, she faced trial by douking. They would tie her thumbs and toes together and then strap her to a special stool. Then she'd be held down under the water. If she drowned she was innocent, but if she survived she was a witch.' He stopped, watching her closely.

'So what happened to the witch then?'

'Why, she was burned at the stake of course.' Not a flicker of a smile or a trace of amusement crossed his face while he delivered the line.

Vanessa wished she could think of something clever to say, but her mind was reeling and she was lost for words. Maggie was suddenly beside her, an arm around her shoulder.

'Well, that was quite an introduction, Daisy.' She put her other hand on the dog's collar. 'Let's put you out during dinner and then I'll introduce everybody properly.' As she turned away, she winked knowingly at Vanessa. 'It's a bit of a mad house around here at times.'

When they were all seated, Maggie served the crab with a little pot of hot garlic butter on the side. Vanessa examined the prehistoric-looking creatures and the instruments of torture which lay beside each plate – a cracker to break the shell and a long hook to get the meat out of the claws. She had never eaten crab before. Looking across at Ronan and Luke's bewildered faces, she couldn't help but laugh out loud.

'Any tips on how to do this?' she said to Maggie.

The bald man had been introduced as Maggie's lifelong friend and neighbour, James Mackay. He was married to the very tall and severe looking woman who hadn't yet spoken. The other brother, Pat Mackay, was not married and not likely to be, given his dour manner, Vanessa thought.

'Let me show you, lass,' James said.

Soon shell was cracking and flying in all directions across the table, much to the children's amusement. Dipped in the warm butter the morsels of crab meat were like nothing Vanessa had ever experienced. She noticed that Pat didn't touch his crab.

'Vanessa reminds me so much of you, Lee, when you first arrived. A determined and meticulous crab-eater too.' James smiled across at Lee.

'I think Vanessa's a natural, actually.' She looked encouragingly at Vanessa, who didn't acknowledge her, but bent further over her plate.

'Remember how stubborn Lee was?'Pat added grumpily. 'She would insist on throwing the remains into the loch.'

'For Nessie,' Vanessa said appreciatively.

'Why, that's exactly what she would say too.'

'Have you ever seen her, Mr Mackay?' Vanessa asked hopefully.

'Nae. Absolute rubbish. Total nonsense of course!' Pat said quickly.

'Oh, don't mind him. He wouldn't believe in his own mother if he hadn't seen her every day for sixty years.' James grinned cheekily at his brother. 'Lots of us 'ere have seen strange things over the years, as did our parents before us.' His gaze settled on Lee before he said quietly, 'It's always when you're least expecting it. Isn't that the truth of it, Lee?'

Vanessa felt the jolt. She hadn't thought about Lee seeing Nessie, that she might have known the secrets of the loch before her. She looked across the table at Lee's open, friendly face and, hoping not to catch her eye, Vanessa waited for her reply. Lee looked thoughtful as if she was about to share something important when Ronan spoke.

'So how does this creature breathe? If she has to come up to the surface for air, she'd be seen all the time.'

'Well put, lad,' Pat egged him on.

'There are caves down there,' Lee answered, 'places with pockets of air. It's nearly 1,000 feet deep in spots, you know. But what if she has gills as well as being an air-breather?'

'That's a believer talking for sure,' Pat said dryly.

'No, the lung-fish can breathe in and out of the water, so why couldn't others adapt?' Lee became animated as she turned on Pat.

'And if you're going to start that stuff about sea creatures not surviving in fresh water, you're wrong there too, Pat. Bull sharks have adapted to the fresh water of Lake Nicaragua. We've seen the occasional seal in Loch Ness. Admit it. Hell, even salmon come up river to the loch. So why not Nessie?'

'Too far-fetched for my tastes. That's all.'

'I thought it was some kind of long lost dinosaur,' James remarked, but before Lee could answer, Pat cut in.

'Well, if it's a cold-blooded dinosaur it'll be bloody cold in that loch.'

'True, except there has been a turnaround by the scientists there too,' Lee said with a smile. 'Most now say that dinosaurs were, in fact, warm-blooded, so that means she could survive in the cold water. If she is a dinosaur, that is.'

'Pah! See, it's all rubbish, even the scientists keep changing their minds.' Pat sat back and crossed his arms across his chest.

'What do you think it is, Lee?' Luke asked.

'Well, the most popular theory is that it's a plesiosaurus – that's a type of aquatic reptile.' Lee spoke to Luke directly. 'And while most plesiosaurus fossils have been found under marine conditions, some have been discovered in places that were fresh water, particularly in rivers and estuaries. So they might well exist in salt and fresh water.'

'Yes, but what do you think?' Vanessa asked abruptly. She blushed to her roots as all eyes turned to look at her.

Lee tilted her head slightly to one side and regarded Vanessa coolly; pausing as if she was deciding how to answer.

'I think she's probably a deep-sea mammal – a type of whale that's evolved to deep water – with a long eel-like neck, flippers ...'

Alan spoke up: 'I think it's unlikely that there's a species of whale that we haven't discovered, given the amount of research these days.'

'Well, until recently, nobody had ever seen the giant squid that lives in the deep,' Lee replied. 'They were the stuff of storybooks until this century, and even now we've only got a dead one that washed up. No one has ever seen it alive.'

'True ... but a new species? That seems a bit of a cop-out, surely?' Alan could not resist a chance to cross-examine, but Lee continued unfazed.

'There are new species of things being discovered all the time, Alan. Think of the coelacanth, a fish they caught alive this century which had been thought to be extinct for sixty-five million years.'

'And how about those sea urchins that turned up on eBay recently? Scientists are now saying that they are a new species.' Vanessa couldn't resist joining in. She glared at her father, just to let him know she was still angry at him and that she hadn't forgiven him. She just wished that she didn't sound as if she was siding with Lee.

'I heard about that,' Lee said excitedly. 'Isn't it amazing?'

'Well, I think you might have to be in your line of work to get excited about that one!' Alan smiled at her in an indulgent way.

Vanessa suddenly realised that she had no idea what Lee did. But there was no way she was going to ask Lee in front of all these people. No way on earth.

'Where are you off to next?' Ronan clearly did know.

Vanessa racked her brains to remember some clue she might have dropped.

'Finnish Lapland. It's interesting but could be tricky. The reindeer are in trouble up there.'

Vanessa was taken aback. That wasn't at all what she had expected.

'Normally they eat the bark off the trees, but food is becoming a real problem for them now that the Finnish government are giving out logging licences to anyone who pays enough.'

Vanessa knew she was staring at Lee. She bit her lip hard before asking, 'So what exactly are you going to do?'

'I'm a zoologist; I work for Greenpeace. I'll be collecting evidence and assessing the impact with other scientists. Then, we will try to arrange talks with the government officials and get them to change their policy on it. It doesn't always work,' she added with a laugh, 'but we have to try.'

Vanessa, who couldn't help feeling impressed, glanced down the table at her father. He was gazing steadily at Lee and the pride in his face struck at her heart.

Vanessa leaned over to Maggie, who was sitting beside her, and said quietly, 'Daisy is going mad outside, Maggie. Will I go and try to calm her?'

'You do that, dear,' she said kindly. 'Her bark is torture isn't it!'

Touching Vanessa's shoulder, she added, 'You take

your time lass, the pudding has been slow-baking in the oven all afternoon, another few minutes will make nae difference at all.'

It was a relief to be outside, away from them all. Vanessa breathed in deeply and stared out into the blackness. The air smelled foreign to her. The vegetation, sweeter than at home, made her light-headed. Surely the water was unnaturally still? Vanessa walked down to the edge where Daisy was barking furiously. She pulled at her collar, but Daisy shook her off and continued barking with an urgency that unnerved her.

'Silly mutt, there's nothing out there,' she said uncertainly.

They stood at the edge of the loch for a few minutes more, Daisy barking, Vanessa searching. But no matter how hard she strained her eyes, Vanessa could see nothing at all. Tired now, she bent down and wrapped her arms around Daisy's neck. The dog stopped barking for a second, pleased with the attention and licked her face. Then she turned back to the loch and barked again.

Vanessa stood up slowly; she'd have to go back in and face them all again. She peered along the bank to the left where she thought the abbey at Fort Augustus should be, but it was too dark to make out except the outline of trees. Tomorrow she would explore it with Daisy and then go out on the loch in the wooden fishing boat Maggie had talked about. Not with Lee, though. She would have this adventure on her own.

CHAPTER 11

In Drumnadrochit in the year 1880, E.H. Bright and his cousin saw a dark grey creature with a long neck come out of a wooded area, waddle to the water's edge and then plunge into the water.

It was ten o'clock before Vanessa stirred the next morning. She lay on in bed feeling very relaxed. The mattress was so much softer than her one at home and the crisp white cotton sheets were pure luxury.

She let her eyes travel slowly around the room, taking in every detail – the polished wooden floors; the pretty wash basin; the table and chair, both painted apple green, that were positioned in front of the window. It looked so inviting, a perfect place for her to do some sketching. She used to draw all the time when her mum was alive. They would take sketchbooks and charcoals with them everywhere. She thought of the terrible charcoal of Nessie on the file cover and smiled wistfully. She would give anything, absolutely anything, to have her mum here for even a minute or two.

There was a soft knock and a pause before Maggie put her head around the door.

'Good morning, dear, did you sleep well?'

'Great, thanks. The bed's so comfortable; I'm finding it hard to get up.'

'Well, why should you? You're on your holidays, stay in it as long as you like. Why don't I bring breakfast up to you?'

'Maybe I could have it at that little table there. I was just thinking about sketching the view, actually.'

'Well, why not?' Maggie must have seen the uncertainty in Vanessa's face. 'You'll need something to draw with, and on, of course.'

She pulled open a door on the opposite wall, revealing a cupboard lined with shelves and full of small wooden boxes and books. Resting on the floor were piles of canvases of all sizes.

'Here we go.' Maggie pulled out a box filled with charcoals and then flicked through a sketchpad to check that there were some free pages. 'You get started and I'll get breakfast. I won't ask you what you want; it will be a Highland surprise!'

'Thanks, Maggie. I love it here,' Vanessa said suddenly, surprising herself. She was rewarded by Maggie's smile and the kindest of looks. 'By the way, the rest of the family are heading off on a fishing trip with Lee to one of the rivers nearby. Do you want to join them or would you prefer to explore a little yourself round about here?'

'Oh, yes, explore, please. That's exactly what I want to do.'

'We are minding Daisy for a few days while James has gone to Glasgow. Maybe you could take her for a walk for me.'

'Are all the Mackays gone away, then?' Vanessa asked.

'No; Laura, his wife, rarely goes out. It's enough that she comes here occasionally for dinner. And Pat simply refuses to walk "the beast", as he calls her.'

'I suppose she might be a bit hyper for him.' Vanessa laughed. What a strange bunch they were!

'You could take Daisy for a walk to Fort Augustus

where the locks are. It's only a couple of minutes along the road.'

'Isn't that the abbey where the monk saw Nessie?'

'Aye, that's true. It's in ruins now, but the cloisters are still lovely. Take your sketchbook. Mind you, it will be hard to get Daisy to explore it with you. She's highly strung at the best of times and she hates that place.'

CHAPTER 12

On 26 May 1934, Brother Richard Horan from St Benedictine's Abbey at Fort Augustus had a very clear sighting. He was working near the abbey boathouse when he heard a noise in the water and looked up to find a creature with a long, graceful neck and seal-like head staring at him. Three other people watching from different positions also saw the same thing.

Vanessa followed the road down the hill into the village. She could see the two spires of Fort Augustus Abbey ahead. Daisy kept straining on her lead, dragging Vanessa off the road and at one point almost into a ditch. But as Vanessa came up to the metal gate into the abbey grounds, she was glad she had brought her – snooping around was far less suspicious if you had a dog in tow.

She pushed the gate, but it didn't move. She pushed hard again and it rattled loudly. It was then that she noticed a large padlock on the inside. Maggie had said it would be no problem to explore the abbey, but now Vanessa felt unsure. Would she have to climb through the gaps or go over the top? What if there was a cranky caretaker on the other side with a shotgun?

All she could see from the road were the spires; the buildings themselves were hidden by trees. It was frustrating to be this close and not see anything. As she stood there, trying to decide what to do, she felt a prickle creep across her skin along the back of her neck and shoulders. It was a strange, but not an unpleasant sensation. It wasn't fear she felt, more like excitement, and she suddenly felt an extraordinary longing to be inside the abbey.

Daisy must have been feeling something too, because she started to whine and push herself up against Vanessa's legs.

Vanessa put her head against the bars of the gate. They were just wide enough to squeeze her head through. The rest of her body followed easily enough. But Daisy wouldn't follow. Although perfectly able, she simply refused to move.

Vanessa remembered a small bread roll she had in her pocket. She held it out through the bars, just out of reach, and it did the trick. Daisy's greed got her through the gate, but Vanessa realised she was going to have to drag her every inch of the way to the abbey. Unless . . .

She spotted a garden bench amongst the trees. Just the thing! She tied Daisy to the arm of the bench. She could finish the bread roll in peace, while Vanessa went on. Thank goodness she had picked it up in the kitchen on her way out. It had been intended as emergency rations, something to eat when she got to the abbey.

Vanessa watched enviously as Daisy gulped it down. She herself was starving. She hadn't eaten a pick of the breakfast Maggie brought up to her. Salty porridge followed by sliced fried black pudding and kippers – what a combination! It had been a nightmare getting rid of it all. The porridge had ended up being washed down the sink, the pudding had found its way into Daisy and the kippers into the loch for Nessie.

As she walked on, Vanessa pulled out the small map that Maggie had given her with the markings for the various buildings of the abbey. Straight ahead stood the monastery with its tower looking out over the loch. The cloistered gardens were directly behind it; to the right stood the old church, and on the left the old school with the remains of a clock tower. She heard a bark in the distance. It didn't sound like Daisy, though, and, anyway, it seemed to come from the wrong direction.

The air was still and smelled unusually sweet. What wild plant gave off such a strong, sweet fragrance, she wondered. It made her feel almost dizzy. There was something familiar about it, but she couldn't remember what. She moved towards the left, hoping to go around the buildings to the front to get a view of the loch, but a couple of times she reached a dead end and had to turn back. She kept going until she saw boat masts ahead. They must be moored in the canal. Maggie had told her the Caledonian Canal was along here by the abbey. The boats were probably waiting to get through the lock-gate to go south to Loch Gairns.

Using the boats as a marker, she soon came to the canal, and then she followed it along towards the loch. Just at the point where the canal met the loch, she came to a pretty little stone tower with a white-painted roof. It didn't have an entrance, though, or not that she could find, which seemed a bit pointless. Vanessa sat on the bank and let her feet dangle above the water. The view across the loch was breathtaking. There were large mountains on both sides and a light wind created shadows and ripples along the surface. She watched the water for any movement, any sign at all of Nessie. Wouldn't it be great if she just appeared now, with nobody else around and in such a beautiful place!

Vanessa turned to look across the lawns in front of the monastery and tried to work out exactly where the monk and his friend had stood when they saw Nessie. She stood up then, and walked towards the building until she found herself almost under the tower.

She was beginning to feel a little strange in herself now, and tired too. Suddenly, a huge black hawk glided out from behind the tower, soaring high above her. She watched in awe – its movement was so graceful. But then the hawk swooped right down towards her, flying terrifyingly close to her head. She ducked, clutching her hair. Was he attacking her? The bird circled, getting ready to come at her again, when Vanessa heard a deep rumble and the sound of bubbling water behind her. She spun on her heels, her heart fluttering in her chest, her breathing suddenly shallow. Before she could register anything at all in the water, a film fell across her eyes and she crumpled to the ground.

Turning on her side, she tried to protect her face. Something was licking it. It took her a while to register that it was Daisy, and that Maggie was stroking her hair, talking to her. For a split second, she imagined she was back in the kitchen at the dinner table, but as she rolled onto her back, she saw the spires of the abbey again, and remembered. How long had she lain there?

'You're white as a sheet, lass. What happened to you? You must have been out cold for ages. I got worried and came after you. Daisy was the first one I found, barking like mad.'

'Oh, Maggie, I am sorry. She wouldn't come any farther so I thought …'

She stopped, suddenly aware of a grinding pain above her eyes as she sat up.

'Headache,' she muttered and struggled to her feet.

'We'll call Doc Morris when we get back. He can look you over.'

'I'm fine, honestly. It was just … hunger. I sometimes feel light-headed on an empty stomach.'

'You can't be hungry after that monster breakfast, surely?

She'd blown it now. 'Oh, well, a little. I have a huge appetite,' she said lamely.

They started to walk back towards the gate again, Maggie linking Vanessa's arm through hers, while Daisy pulled hard on the lead.

'Double rations tomorrow for you then, my girl.' Maggie was clearly puzzled at the thought that her famous Highland breakfast was not enough to satisfy this slip of a girl.

CHAPTER 13

Alex Campbell, a water bailiff on Loch Ness for many decades and a local correspondent for the Inverness Courier, *saw the monster many times. In May 1934, he said 'a strange object seemed to shoot out of the calm waters almost opposite the Abbey boathouse'. He reckoned that the head and neck stood about 6 feet above the water and the body, a large rounded hump, was about 30 feet long. It was like no animal he had ever seen before.*

It was dark, pitch dark, when Vanessa opened her eyes with a start. What had woken her? She listened, straining to hear any noise at all. The silence in the room was almost like a physical presence, something heavy and breathless. Vanessa didn't move, her arms felt rigid by her sides, her neck taut. She waited until her eyes started to adjust to the dark.

Gradually, she could make out the window that looked out over Loch Ness, but farther from the end of her bed than she had remembered. Was it always curved at the top? She peered harder, trying to focus. The window in her room had four small panes, didn't it?

Her legs felt wobbly when she put them over the side of her bed and stood up slowly. She walked towards the window and reached out to feel the glass. But there was none, instead she felt a light cool breeze flutter about her hand and she drew it back to her chest as if nursing a pain. Turning to look back at her bed, she found instead four rough stone walls and a staircase in one corner. Her bed was gone.

Panicked now, she looked back out through the open arch to the water. She was sure it was Loch Ness, but where was the red boat, Maggie's rowing boat? Tense and alert, her eye caught a dark shape to the right on the grass below and she leaned forward to try and make it out.

Blinking hard and nervously, she watched the

shape move slowly towards the water's edge. All of a sudden, it made sense to her: she was looking at the dark robes of a monk and his head was covered by a cowl. The figure stopped, he seemed to be surrounded by a small pool of light that came from beyond him. She found it hard to drag her eyes away, but she let her gaze dart out beyond him to the source of the light in the water. Previously an inky black space, she watched as the blackness lifted in one spot. Light seemed to be coming from beneath the water and rising to the surface. Gradually, the light became stronger and then a little more coloured, dull green and brackish yellow, luminescent.

Vanessa knew her limbs were incapable of any movement. She could feel the air in her nostrils with each inhalation, her scalp taut with fear. The world stood still and she waited. And then she saw her.

Nessie's head broke through the surface and for what seemed like an eternity, she held her neck high and looked towards Vanessa. She felt a warm rush of pleasure break like a wave inside her. She was looking at Nessie – her mother's dream had come true.

Time stood still.

Then she saw the monk raise his right hand as if in

a blessing or a salute to the magnificent creature and, to her dismay, the scene slowly began to fold in on itself, the colours caving, once again, into blackness.

CHAPTER 14

On 14 April 1933, Mr and Mrs John Mackay, the owners of the Drumnadrochit Hotel on Loch Ness were driving home when they saw a disturbance on the loch surface. They watched 'an enormous animal rolling and plunging' for several minutes until it disappeared in a great upsurge of water. Their story appeared in the Inverness Courier, *2 May 1933.*

Vanessa woke to a definite noise this time. There was someone at her door. Glancing at her watch, she saw that it was ten o'clock. Why was she sleeping so long and so late these days? The soft knock came again and she realised that Maggie was probably standing outside with a huge breakfast. What would she do with it this time? She would have to divide it into small stashes, wrapped in tissue, and get rid of it slowly over the day.

When she opened the door, it was the last person on earth she expected to see – Lee.

'Oh, it's you,' she said ungraciously. 'I didn't mean it like that,' she stumbled on, realising how rude it had sounded. 'It's just that I was expecting Maggie. She brought me breakfast yesterday.'

'So I heard. I also heard that you almost fainted with hunger a few hours later, so I guessed you felt the same about her breakfasts as I did growing up.' And with that she pushed an oval tray into Vanessa's hands. When Vanessa looked down she saw, to her delight, a tray filled with all her favourite breakfast things – white toast with butter and marmalade, a bowl of Rice Krispies, fresh orange juice and a huge cup of hot chocolate. She looked up at Lee and grinned with delight.

'She won't be offended?' she asked Lee.

'She won't know,' Lee answered mischievously. 'I just said I'd bring you breakfast this morning. Indeed, she'd be mortally wounded if she ever found out we hated salted porridge and haggis.'

'And did she never guess?'

'Goodness gracious no! I could never bear to hurt her feelings. She was so sure that I'd love Scotland and love their food when I arrived from America to live with them.'

'And did you?' Vanessa asked with genuine interest.

'Loved Scotland, still hate the food! But don't ever tell her. Well, I'd better see to the others. See you later.'

'Thanks, Lee.' It was the first time Vanessa had used Lee's name, and it felt strange on her tongue. She was sure she saw Lee start slightly when she said it.

Vanessa ate her breakfast at the table by the window. She stared hard at the water and the grass below, picturing the monk, the colours and trying to visualise Nessie in front of her. It was frustrating, though: the sun, clear skies and mirror-like water made too much of a contrast to let her recall the scene properly.

By the time she had finished, it was almost half past eleven, so she dressed and went down to the kitchen. It was empty except for Daisy, who gave her an exuberant welcome. She eventually settled the dog down again by giving her a piece of ham that she found in the fridge, and made a quick getaway into the garden. That dog wasn't the easy canine companion you'd want. She was like one of those friends that talked incessantly – interesting, but exhausting.

Vanessa found everyone gathered down near the end of the lawn bent over a pile of boxes, and she could see a number of fishing rods on the grass. Luke and Ronan were in their element.

'Vanessa, wait until you see this kit,' Ronan said, when he spotted her. 'It's fantastic.'

'Look at this one!' Luke held up a rather ordinary rod and waved it in Vanessa's direction.

'Ghillie's Choice, one of the finest Clan Rods,' Maggie offered, 'as used by the Prince of Wales.'

Let me guess – Lee's rod with which she won every angling competition there ever was in the Highlands, Vanessa thought.

It was as if Maggie had read her mind. 'They belonged to my husband, Peter. He won lots of competitions in his lifetime. All the cups in the sitting room cabinet are his.'

'Oh, right. I noticed those yesterday,' Vanessa said lamely. She was flushed with embarrassment.

'Are you going fishing again?' Vanessa asked nobody in particular.

'Well, Luke and Ronan are going to fish in Loch Ness and Lee and I ...' Alan started to explain.

'But is there anything to catch in it?' Ronan interrupted.

'Of course, lad!' Maggie exclaimed before Alan could reply. 'The loch has tons of fish – brown trout, sea trout, arctic char. And you might even still get a few salmon, although it's late in the season. The best spot on the loch is around the bend there at Bell's Point. It's the Mackay's land so there's nae a problem.'

Ronan and Luke looked pleased.

'Vanessa, I've given the boys the choice of staying here to fish, or coming with Lee and me to visit Lorrie on the Isle of Skye. That's Lee's grandmother,' Alan added when he saw her blank look. 'What would you like to do?'

'Fish,' she said shortly. She couldn't believe that he was going off with her again. Family holiday, my foot.

'Can we take the boat out?' Luke asked. 'We're all good swimmers.'

'Absolutely not,' Maggie said without hesitation. 'The winds can get up suddenly on the loch. And no swimming either, the eels are big out there.'

'When we get back, maybe Lee could take you out,' Alan said looking at Lee for support.

'Of course, I'd love to. I'll show you all the nooks and crannies on the south end that only the locals know.'

The boys agreed eagerly enough, but Vanessa said nothing.

'We'll be back by half past four. Make sure you catch us something for dinner.'

'So we'll go out in the boat at half four?' Vanessa demanded, examining Luke's rod closely.

'No problem.' Alan was clearly relieved with the outcome. He picked up a rod in three pieces and began its construction. 'Will you look in the box for a reel, Vanessa, and this one can be yours?'

They found their way easily enough to Bell's Point. It was a thin piece of land that jutted into the loch and at the end was a small whitewashed round bollard. The boys laughed and joked about whether it was something used to tie up boats, a viewing platform for Nessie hunters or a very tiny bell tower, as Luke suggested. In the end, Ronan decided that it was a leprechaun perch and sat himself on top with his fishing rod.

Within the next couple of hours, they caught a few

fish, all of which were tiny and were returned immediately to the water. Maggie had packed them a picnic, but Vanessa eyed it uncertainly. It looked pretty, bound up in a blue and white check cloth, but knowing Maggie it could be that haggis stuff again. She unpacked it to find small bundles in grease proof paper tied with string.

'Anyone hungry yet?' Vanessa shouted. 'It's nearly half past one, you know.'

'OK, you put the stuff out and we'll – ' Luke stopped mid-sentence, his face lit up. 'I've definitely got something bigger this time.' He started to reel it in.

Vanessa watched with a smile on her face. Luke was pretty cool really. So many of her friends complained about their horrible teenage brothers and how mean they were. She felt the lump in her throat. If she was being honest, it was she who was horrible to him … and to Ronan sometimes.

She busied herself by unpacking the picnic onto the cloth which she spread out on the grass, but she was still thinking about her brothers. Why did she give them such a hard time? They had lost their mother too.

And then something that she had never thought of before struck her. It seemed to reverberate and gather intensity in her head and she knew that it was true. She was angry with Luke and Ronan, angry that they were able to cope so well with their mother's death. Of course they cried and still had their bad days, but they were OK. She knew suddenly that she was not only angry with them, but envious of them too.

It seemed to Vanessa that the pain which seared through her on the day they buried her mother had not lessened even for a moment. She remembered standing over the deep grave and throwing the soil on the coffin, she could hear the scattering of the earth in her head. But worse came as they left the graveyard: the feeling that they were all deserting her. She could never forgive herself or them for that.

Since then, she had felt adrift, disconnected from everyone and everything. Her friends talked about the future and what they would do – where they would go next week, what they would do next summer, even about university. Vanessa tried her best to act the same, but it felt as if life had stopped that day. There was only her past now and no future for her at all. She dreaded everything ahead – her next birthday, the third Christmas without her mother, going into secondary school, getting her period. Who would help her through all that?

'Look, look, Vanessa. Luke's caught a huge one.' Ronan was almost dancing with excitement as the fish was landed. Vanessa restrained herself from saying anything – bigger, it was; huge, it wasn't.

'What is it, Luke?' Vanessa asked instead.

'A trout, I think. It's large enough to eat, so we'll bring it back and cook it later.'

He put the fish into a bag filled with ice that Maggie had given them. 'OK, so what's for lunch?'

They all stared at the tablecloth laid out on the grass, Vanessa seeing the contents for the first time herself.

'At last, a proper Famous Five picnic!' Luke said. 'Freshly baked bread, sliced sweet tomatoes, farmhouse cheese, cold sausages and to top it all, George …? ' He looked at Vanessa expectantly.

'What?' she said sternly. 'And I'm not George, I'd rather be Timmy the dog than that cranky insecure girl/boy thing.'

'I'm Dick,' Ronan said quickly.

'So where's the ginger beer, Timmy?'

Vanessa checked the basket again.

'None, sorry. Aunt Fanny has failed us badly this time.'

The boys decided to stay on fishing for a little while longer, but after lunch Vanessa went back to the cottage. Despite the lovely afternoon, she felt strangely despondent. It was hard to put one foot in front of the other and she desperately needed to sleep. She hoped that Maggie wouldn't be in the kitchen; she didn't want to talk to anyone.

Once inside the cottage, Vanessa scurried quickly up the stairs, trying to make her footsteps light on the creaking boards. She washed her hands and face in cold water and then lay down on her bed. She wondered if she would have the same dream again, and this time maybe she would get a longer look at Nessie.

Twenty minutes later, she was still awake. Her eyes roamed around the room and came to a stop at the cupboard that Maggie had got the charcoals and sketchpad from.

She opened both doors wide. It was clearly a much loved space. Labelled boxes lined the shelves – Water colour paints, Oils, Pastels, Brushes. Her eyes flew along the rows and then stopped at one labelled Loch Ness articles.

Vanessa looked back over her shoulder to the closed bedroom door. She knew she was being nosy; something she despised in others and usually had no problem resisting herself. But this time something compelled her, and it felt too important to ignore.

Sliding out the box, she opened the top and lifted up the first article. It was a copy of the *Northern Chronicle,* dated June 1930. 'A Strange Experience on Loch Ness.' She scanned the page. It was about local fishermen who had seen a large creature cause a disturbance in the water near Tore Point. It finished by asking if readers could help enlighten them on the subject. The next few articles were ones received over the following weeks in reply. Her eye caught another from the *Inverness Courier,* dated 2 May 1933. 'A Strange Spectacle on Loch Ness' by Alex Campbell. Vanessa read quickly through the opening paragraph.

'Mr and Mrs John Mackay, owners of the local Inn at Drumnadrochit …'

She started at the name, Mackay – weren't they the neighbours, the odd brothers, she had met on their first night? Her mind ran furiously over conversations trying to remember their names – Pat was the cranky one with the wild white hair, but what was the bald one called? Hang on. If he was even twenty years old in 1933, that would make him over a hundred now. Maybe John Mackay was their father. She remembered them talking about their mother. James – that was the bald one's name! He was the one who believed in Nessie and had talked about sightings, but Pat had dismissed it altogether.

Vanessa rifled through the rest hungrily, scanning the dates and headings. They were all in meticulous chronological order. And there were hundreds of them. It would be days of reading. What if she started with the last article, the most recent one? Having found it, however, she was disappointed, as the last article proved to be nothing about the Loch Ness Monster. Dated 7 May 1986 and in the *Inverness Courier*, it appeared to be about a local child, Lena Cook, who had gone missing, and there was an appeal to the community for information.

A creak on the stairs made Vanessa jump guiltily. She closed the box quickly and shut the cupboard doors as quietly as possible. She waited, but the footsteps continued past her door without hesitation and she heard another door close down the corridor. Vanessa felt a tightness in her chest. Asthma or panic? She sat on the side of the bed again and tried to breathe evenly; she hadn't had an asthma attack in about five years. Her mind was racing but her eyes kept being drawn back to the closed cupboard doors. What else would she find in there?

This time she looked at the piles of canvases stacked on the floor. They were all facing inwards. She would need to move a couple of things in front of them to be able to turn them around and get a proper look. Maybe they were all blank on the other side. She paused a moment, undecided about moving things. This was serious snooping. She would absolutely hate anyone, especially a stranger, rearranging her personal stuff.

When she turned the first and the largest canvas around, the shock was so great that she actually dropped it. The thud was soft enough but she was terrified someone had heard it and would come to investigate. When there was no sound, she picked it up again and held it tightly. Her hands were shaking.

The colours and light were exactly as she had seen them, but the detail of Nessie's face was much clearer – smooth skin and almost seal-like eyes. They were intelligent eyes, but she looked anxious, even threatened, Vanessa thought. But it was the monk in the cowl that really spooked her. That had been her dream, hadn't it? Who had painted it and when had they done it? Perhaps she had walked in her sleep the first night, saw the picture and then dreamt about it the second night? It sounded ridiculous to her, but then the alternative was even more unbelievable.

CHAPTER 15

On 22 July 1933, when Mr and Mrs Spicer were returning home after a holiday in Scotland, their car nearly hit a huge creature as it slithered across the road into the loch. The 'prehistoric animal' as Mrs Spicer described it, was very ugly: about 6 to 8 feet long with a tall neck and a high back. In a letter to the Inverness Courier *published in 1933, Mr Spicer said:'Whatever it is, and it may be a land and water animal, I think it should be destroyed, as I am not sure, if I had been quite so close to it, whether I should have cared to tackle it. It is difficult to give you a better description, as it moved so swiftly and the whole thing was sudden. There is no doubt it exists.'*

Vanessa turned over the rest of the canvases quickly and positioned them in a circle around her. They were all different images of Nessie moving through the water. Her skin was generally a charcoal grey but in some pictures, it had a definite green tinge. The fins looked similar to a whale's, except for the second smaller set of fins at the back. Maybe they were the residual limbs of a sea mammal that was also once a land creature. The elongated tail and neck were more like that of the deep-sea eel. Perhaps their theory had been right after all, and Nessie was some form of deep-sea-adapted mammal. Well, why not? The beaked whale lives in deep oceans and can dive to 1,000 feet.

Vanessa whooped quietly for joy and the intensity of her excitement made her feel if as she might explode in the confines of the small cupboard. Suddenly, she felt very sure about Nessie – she was a sea creature that came into the loch when she was small and got trapped. That's why the real sightings only happened after the building of the Caledonian Canal. She had seen Nessie herself – at least in her dream or premonition or whatever it was. But whoever had painted these pictures knew the monster very well indeed.

Vanessa looked at her watch. It was twenty to five. Her dad had said that Lee would take them out in the boat on Loch Ness at half past four. It was time to go – with or without Lee. If she waited much longer it would get too dark.

She pulled on her jacket over her warm fleece and went downstairs. There was no sign of the boys or of Maggie, thank God. The air was crisp and cool when she stepped into the garden and the boat was sitting quite still in the water. It was like a millpond, perfectly safe. She would take it out 50 metres or so around the corner and probably be back in before Alan and Lee arrived home.

She untied the boat easily enough and pushed off with the oar. To her dismay, she found that she wasn't a very good rower. It was usually Luke or her dad who rowed when they went fishing in Ireland.

Vanessa put the oars in the oarlocks and pulled hard. They were surprisingly heavy and too deep in the water to pull. They should be closer to the surface, she decided, but when she tried that, she skimmed the top of the water and splashed herself. It took a couple of minutes to work out, but soon she managed a few small but even strokes and moved off from the bank. Keeping the rhythm going, she felt very pleased with herself. It was really quite easy when you got the hang of it. Once she rounded the corner, out of sight of the cottage, her determination evaporated. Dad would kill her if he caught her.

The silence was eerie out on the loch. She had expected to see birds or other boats on the water, but there was nothing. All she could hear was the gentle lap of water on the oars. Every muscle in her body felt rigid as she crouched over, sweating with the effort, trying to decide whether to continue or to go back.

Something moved at great speed from behind the bank of trees, making Vanessa look up with a start. The hawk again – silent and predatory, it circled high over the boat. She felt sure it was the same one that had frightened her in the abbey before. Had it been watching and waiting for her? She stretched her neck backwards, following its every move, terrified it would swoop down on her again. And then she saw it dive and lift a small fish in its beak, soaring back up high into the sky and off behind the trees. How ridiculous she was being! It was simply a hawk, doing what hawks do.

Vanessa tightened her grip on the left oar and then noticed that the right oar was gone. She must have let go as she watched the hawk. Standing up cautiously in the boat, she looked around in the water for it. Relieved, she saw that it was floating about 3 metres away to the right. She could easily punt over to it.

It was slower progress than Vanessa imagined and she could feel a small knot of anxiety in her chest. She would be fine, she told herself. The last thing she needed now was an asthma attack. She couldn't swim to the oar, as she would never be able to get back in the boat, so she would just have to paddle slowly.

It seemed as if the oar was drifting away at exactly the same speed as she was moving towards it. The gap just wouldn't close. She was quite a distance from Maggie's now, and nobody could see her even if they were out in the garden. No panicking, just paddle harder she told herself.

Finally, Vanessa's efforts paid off. Using the other oar she pulled the one in the water in to the side of the boat. It would be difficult to get it up out of the water. Her hands were aching and her left palm was beginning to blister. She stood up again and with less caution this time leaned over the side of the boat, balancing on her stomach to pull it up.

In that moment, as Vanessa balanced on the edge, not wanting to let go of the oar again, she saw what would happen before it actually did. In slow motion, the boat tipped further over under her weight, and she slipped silently into the water, head first. The heavy wooden boat turned turtle on top of her. It made a dull thud, there was no splash, and no shout as Vanessa went under.

CHAPTER 16

There are many strange things about Loch Ness. Locals say that it never gives up its dead. A number of people who drowned have literally disappeared and their bodies have never been found. Even dead fish don't come to the surface.

Vanessa did not feel the blow to the side of her head. It was numbed too quickly by the shock of cold water as her whole body went down. It was icy cold and painful on her skin. She tried to swim, hoping she was going up towards the surface. Her coat and shoes felt like lead weights and the pull downwards was almost overwhelming, but she kicked furiously until her face broke the surface. The moment of relief was intense, but it did not last. Why was it pitch black? Where was she?

Bewildered and tired from kicking to keep afloat, her flaying arms hit out and she grazed her knuckles on something. Yes, the boat of course. She could feel the upside-down bench and the oarlocks: she was beneath the upturned boat. She'd have to go under again to swim out of the boat and do it quickly, because she would soon be too cold to move.

Vanessa groped along the inside edge of the boat. Her clothes were waterlogged and her hands were numb with the cold. She was finding it hard to hold on. She went under and swam hard. The cold bit at her face and scalp, but she gasped with relief to be out in the air. She turned towards the bank.

'Help!' she croaked. She cleared her throat and tried to yell louder, but it made her cough hard. Even to her ears, it was a pitiful cry that wouldn't be heard more than a couple of feet away. Could she swim to the shore? Normally, she could swim that distance with no problem, but her body ached with exhaustion. She couldn't even get a hold on the upturned boat. It was too slimy.

Seconds felt like hours and she knew she wouldn't

be able to cling to the surface much longer. Her limbs were getting heavier and her head lighter. She waited for something to happen, knowing that she couldn't make it happen herself.

She felt her vision blur and she blinked furiously. Her mind was blank with panic and her body weak with effort. Nobody could save her.

'Mum, help me. Help me please …' Her voice was barely a whisper.

Was she imagining things? She felt the warmth creep over her and envelop her body. Her legs and arms, so tense and heavy, began to loosen slowly.

She registered the glow of light beneath her, just seconds before she sank down deep into Loch Ness.

CHAPTER 17

On 30 July 1979, Alistair and Sue Boyd parked in a spot above Temple Pier when they saw a huge hump surface in the loch. It was about the size of a yacht hull, but by the time they got their camera from the car, it had disappeared.

When Vanessa woke the first time, it was dark. From behind half-shut eyes and the filter of her lashes, she tried to make out some shapes. It was a vague blur and her brain registered nothing familiar. Her eyelids felt heavy as they closed over. She was too tired to fight sleep.

The second time she opened them wide, she lay

very still and looked straight ahead. Green. She rolled her head a little to the left and then the right. There appeared to be a soft green glow in the air all around her. Her hands and feet felt quite numb and her back ached. She wriggled slightly, testing her limbs, suddenly aware that she was lying on something extremely hard and uncomfortable. None of it made sense. Perhaps if she closed her eyes again, the dream would fade like the last time and she would find herself back in bed. Willingly, her eyelids shut the world out for a second time.

She didn't know how much actual time had passed before she came to properly. This time, she pulled herself up to a sitting position and looked around. Above her the stone ceiling arched like a cathedral roof and she saw a number of openings in the walls. Were there caves up there? she wondered. Looking down now she found that she was sitting on a ledge about 2 feet above the water, which shone an extremely odd shade of green. She lay down on her stomach and dipped her hand in, it was cool but not cold and she made ripples with her fingers. She watched the movement of the water around her hands and was quite unprepared for the sudden desire to get into the water that overwhelmed her. As she took off her socks and shoes, she noticed that it was the walls rather than the water that were glowing green. Was it some kind of algae? She lay on her stomach, hanging out quite far over the edge and peered into the deep as if it had some intense connection with her. The glow from the walls beneath the water allowed her to see down quite deep. She couldn't be certain, but it looked as if the caves continued beneath the water. She scraped a little of the green algae off the walls and then sat up to examine it. She had seen something like it in the *Blue Planet* series on deep-sea creatures. Bioluminescence, that was it. She remembered being astonished by the tricks of evolution that help in survival. Wasn't it the hatchet fish that lived in the ocean at 4,500 feet? Not only did it glow, but it could change its brightness to attract prey or to camouflage it. And didn't some jellyfish have to eat plants or algae to keep their glow?

Why don't you try some?

Vanessa looked up, startled, as the sound of a voice echoed through her head. She was sure it hadn't been spoken out loud. It had felt more like a reverberation inside her skull. A prickling fear crept through her, tightening every muscle in her body. She listened for any sound at all and, hearing only silence, she forced herself to stand up and look around. Should she shout out and see if anyone answered? She opened her mouth wide, but no sound came out. Stunned, she tried again, but no attempt to clear her throat or cough would produce any sound at all.

She stood very still for a while, holding her breath for long periods and then breathing as quietly as she could in between. Looking up above her, Vanessa scanned the walls for any shaft of light that might show a way out. But all the time, she kept being distracted in her thoughts by the water below, drawing her in. Trying hard to think about where she might be or how she got there, Vanessa felt her mind go blank. It was a pleasant sensation – calm and peaceful. True, she couldn't remember where she was or what had happened just minutes before, but did it matter?

Tired all of a sudden, she sat down and tried to reach the water with her toes. They dangled just out of reach of the surface. Time to dive in, she thought to herself. Time? What time was it? Glancing at her watch, she stopped in her tracks. What had happened to it? Why was the glass broken? It was difficult to see the hands, but it looked as though they had stopped at five o'clock. Morning or evening? A sudden image of herself in the rowing boat flashed through her mind, but before she could register it properly, it slipped away again. She felt frustrated more than afraid now, wondering when she would wake up from this weird and disjointed dream.

Vanessa knew that time must be marching on as she sat and waited for something. For what, she didn't know, just for something. But as there was no change in light and no second hand ticking on her watch, she had no sense of time passing. Eventually, she lay back down on the rock, and making a pillow with her fleece behind her head, she closed her eyes.

CHAPTER 18

On 13 October 1971, Police Sergeant George Mackenzie and Inspector Henry Henderson were with a group who watched two humps moving in the loch at about 10 to 15 mph. They guessed that the creature was about 30 to 40 feet long. 'It was obvious that the two objects were part of one large animate object,' Inspector Henderson is said to have reported.

It was dark by the time Alan pulled the car into the driveway at Heather Cottage. He turned off the engine and sat quietly with his hands resting on the steering wheel. Without looking at Lee, his hand sought hers.

'Thank you. That was one of the nicest days I have had in a long time.'

Lee started to reply but Alan, lost in his own thoughts, continued determinedly.

'Lee, you've been so good to us all, so understanding. It's difficult …' Alan stumbled over his words. 'It can be a little difficult, I know … with Vanessa …'

'Of course, it's unbelievably difficult for her, Alan.' Lee sounded more brisk than she intended. 'I remember all too well what it's like when your parents die.'

Alan looked at her startled.

'God, Lee, I know you do. I'm sorry, I didn't mean …'

Lee opened the car door and stood out. She waited until Alan got out and he looked at her across the roof. To his relief, she smiled at him.

'I'm not upset, Alan. It's all a long time ago for me. I'm just saying I understand Vanessa more than you or she thinks.'

Alan squeezed her hand in his as they walked up to the cottage door. The windows on either side of the front door were lit up and the cottage looked so welcoming.

'I love it here, Lee. I feel as if everything will come right eventually.' Alan looked out at the loch and said absently, 'Too late to go out in the boat now.'

'We'll go out early tomorrow instead,' Lee agreed.

'Our second last day,' Alan added, and Lee could hear the tinge of sadness in his voice.

'It's even better here in early summer. We'll come back then.'

Alan smiled back at her fondly. 'It's a gift, you know.' And when Lee looked at him in puzzlement, he added, 'To always say the right thing, I mean.'

They could hear the sound of the television on in the sitting room. There was a fire already lit and the cat had taken up a most comfortable position on Ronan's knee. A sci-fi programme was on and Maggie was busy with her knitting in the corner of the sofa.

'Hi, guys, good fishing?' Alan asked.

'Oh, Dad, it was fantastic. I caught one this size.' Ronan used his hands exuberantly to show the size and in doing so banged the cat, who rose disdainfully and jumped heavily to the floor.

'Maggie says it's a trout.'

Alan looked around.

'Where's Vanessa? Did she fish with you?'

There was silence, the boys once again engrossed in the TV programme.

'Oh, she did, Alan, but the boys said she got tired of it and she went up to her room earlier in the afternoon.' It was Maggie who answered him.

'I'll go up and see her. Are we having fish for supper then?' He laughed. 'I'll cook tonight, Maggie. It's your night off.'

Alan took the stairs two at a time. He was thinking hard about his excuse for being late and the plan for the loch trip tomorrow morning.

He knocked on Vanessa's bedroom door but there was no answer. He paused before knocking again. Perhaps she was asleep. He turned to go down the stairs, and then hesitated with his hand on the banisters. It was half past five. It was late enough if she had slept in the afternoon. Time she got up. He turned back and knocked again, louder this time, but there was still no response. Slowly, he pushed open the door and walked into the bedroom.

CHAPTER 19

On 2 February 1959, AA patrolman Mr Hamish Mackintosh saw something out of this world – 'as if a dinosaur had reared up out of the loch'. He saw a broad, humped body, greyish in colour, with a thin neck and head, as tall as 8 feet above the water, moving towards the shore. He was joined by a local from a nearby house and they watched it together for about five minutes. Mr Mackintosh is believed to have said that he would never go out on Loch Ness in a small boat again.

Alan tried not to look too concerned when he returned to the sitting room. There was a heated debate going on between Luke and Lee about the

X-Files. Alan waited for a break in the intense discussion but it progressed rapidly to the existence of Area 51 and the possibility of alien abduction.

'Well, that might account for your sister's absence, I suppose,' Alan interrupted.

Luke looked at his father with a mildly puzzled face.

'She's not in her room,' he explained.

The boys looked blankly at him.

'She's probably taken her sketchpad out to the garden,' Maggie offered.

'It's dark out there. Why would she do that?' Ronan said, direct as ever.

'Good point.'

'I'll just pop outside and have a look.' Alan moved quickly down the hall into the kitchen and yanked open the back door. Nothing stirred, the air was suspiciously still. Lee joined him without a word and the two of them walked into the garden and down to the water's edge.

'Vancssa!' Alan called. And when he got no answer he raised his voice. 'Vanessa! Are you there? It's dinner time.'

Nothing.

'Vanessa, it's time to come in.' A touch of panic now lifted the edges of his voice, but there was still no answer.

'She's probably just gone for a walk with Daisy. I didn't see her in the house either.'

'Of course, that's probably it.' There was relief in Alan's voice, but he added crossly, 'I'll kill her if she's wandered off without saying anything to Maggie or the boys. She knows she's not allowed. It's not as if she even knows the area.'

As they turned back up to the house, they met Maggie coming through the kitchen door.

'Perhaps Vanessa took Daisy for another walk, Maggie?' Lee took Maggie's hand in hers and they stood facing each other for a second before she answered.

'No. James arrived this morning and took the dog back home, thank God. The daft mutt.'

The silence that followed was awkward, nobody wanting to admit out loud that Vanessa was actually missing at this stage.

'OK, let's go back in to the boys and we'll find out who saw her last.' Maggie took charge. 'We'd better just check every room in the house first in case she's fallen asleep reading or sketching. Then, we'll get torches and do the garden properly.'

Nobody mentioned Loch Ness.

CHAPTER 20

The waters of Loch Ness are darkened by peat particles so that nothing can be seen below 20 or 30 feet. It explains why photography and diving in the loch is so difficult. Sonar equipment has detected large, solid, living objects, bigger than fish or seals, but this technique cannot make out detail, so a creature like Nessie could stay well hidden in the depths.

Vanessa felt the algae in her hands. Was it algae or wet moss? She couldn't decide. It looked like algae but felt more like moss in her hands – spongy, with no smell at all. When Vanessa put it in her mouth it felt curiously natural to her. The taste was unsurprising –

bland, almost grass-like. But when she took the moulded ball out of her mouth to examine it before swallowing it she was amazed at the intensity of the glow. It was as if chewing it had released energy.

You'll need more.

Vanessa started and swallowed hard. The voice in her head was by far the most disturbing feature of all in this dream. Everything else, although odd, was surprisingly comforting, and she felt no fear.

You'll need to eat more to explore the waters.

She felt compelled to obey, using her nails to scrape another handful off the cave wall and chewing dutifully.

More.

This was getting ridiculous. How could she stop it? Vanessa willed herself not to, but her hand reached out to scrape more moss.

It was some time before she began to notice the changes in herself. Normally a light golden brown, the skin on her hands began to look increasingly pale and sickly. She watched mesmerised as her arms slowly took on a greenish colour and then began to glow. Rolling up her trouser legs, she discovered that her feet and legs were turning green too.

Now take a swim and see the difference.

Slowly she stood up and looked below her into the water. She could see down near the edges with the glow from the moss, but farther out it was dull and murky. Why couldn't she be dreaming about turquoise-blue Mediterranean waters? She dived in, breaking the surface of the water with only the slightest ripple.

The water felt cool and refreshing as she expected, but something else surprised her. It also felt soft and velvety, almost as if it were caressing her. She raised her hand out of the water and let it drip through her fingers, trying to understand the feeling of healing and comfort it gave her. When she put her hand back into the water, the glow from her skin was intense and she could see right down below her into the depths. There were no fish or plants, nothing at all to see.

She took a deep breath and went under, swimming down hard. About 10 feet below the surface she could see a series of caves but she didn't feel like exploring them. Deeper again she thought she saw something move, so she swam towards it, but it was gone by the time she reached the spot.

She looked back up to the surface; it seemed a long way off. How had she managed to hold her breath so long? She was a good swimmer, but thirty seconds was about her best breath hold. Luke was much better. Luke. The name sang in her head, reverberating. It felt so familiar and yet she couldn't attach an image to the name.

When she got to the surface again, Vanessa climbed out. She felt tired and hungry now. Something had disturbed her equilibrium, some memory she couldn't place. She scraped some more moss off the walls and put this fresh supply in her sock, which began to glow comically. She giggled at the sight of it, feeling happier again. She sat now on her fleece and examined her green limbs in awe. Her trousers should have been dripping wet – she'd just climbed out of the water – but they felt dry and comfortable, and her fleece, too, was soft and warm. Presumably this dream would end some time soon. But not too soon, she hoped.

CHAPTER 21

Mr P. Macnab, county councillor and bank manager in Ayrshire, photographed Nessie near Urquhart Castle. The picture was published in the Weekly Scotsman *in October 1958. Far from seeking publicity, he said, 'through diffidence and fear of ridicule, I have kept it to myself until now'.*

Luke and Ronan!

The names popped out of nowhere into her head and she sat up suddenly, grazing her elbow off a rock. Of course, her brothers. How could she have forgotten her brothers? She focused hard and managed to see them on a bank with fishing rods, but beyond that one image she couldn't picture them, no matter how hard she tried.

She looked around, surprised to find herself in the same place. What on earth was this all about? She had never had to find a way out of a dream before. Normally, she just woke up. She looked at her watch, forgetting that it was broken. Five o'clock. Why was that time significant? What had she done to break her watch? She waited for an image, but nothing came. She would find her own way out, even if her mind wasn't willing to help. She jumped to her feet.

The rocks felt almost warm to her touch this time. Her hands and feet were still glowing but very faintly now; she must have been asleep for some time. She gathered more moss into her sock and tucked it into her belt. She knew that she would have to eat some more of it if she wanted to find a way out in the water. Besides she was beginning to like the feel of it on her tongue. First, she would climb up to some of the higher caves and see if there was a tunnel which would lead up to the top. Lead up to the top? Vanessa was puzzled by the thought. What was at the top?

She began to climb quickly. Although her feet were bare, she was sure-footed. She loved climbing. She stopped, picturing herself scaling a large tree. Her lime tree. Of course, in her garden. The images stopped as abruptly as they started.

The teasing memory made her all the more determined, and she climbed up higher past two caves. She didn't stop at either, as she could see the back of them, and there were no tunnels leading anywhere. She paused and looked over to the left at another opening. For some reason, it looked more interesting, even though it was still above her eye level and she couldn't see the back of it. Was she right in thinking that it wasn't as dark up there? Maybe it was the light from an opening. The climb up and across would be more difficult. There were fewer footholds and bigger rocks jutting out and in the way.

She lost her footing just for a moment, scraping her knee on the rock. It didn't hurt at all, but she could see the tear in her jeans and the blood oozing. Do you bleed in your dreams? she wondered. Should she look for a way out through the water instead? She longed to throw herself off the ledge into the water below where she knew she would feel secure and comfortable. Why was the water so appealing?

Water heals.

Perhaps, she thought as the words reverberated in her head. But heals what?

She climbed onto the ledge with some difficulty

and sat on her knees looking around. How disappointing! There was no way out after all, just another cave. Well, not quite just another cave. This one was different, because the bottoms of the walls were lined with the glowing moss. Nearly all the other moss she'd seen or eaten had been at water level or just below it. None of the neighbouring caves was glowing. Strange, that. What made this one different? There was something more to it than just the moss. She could feel something close to her.

Vanessa shuffled along the ground towards the back of the cave, and it was at the very back that she saw a pile of rocks in the shape of a pyramid. The roof of the cave was higher there and she could stand up. The construction had been carefully made, each rock balanced one on top of the other. Who could have built it? As she removed a large one for a closer look, she heard a loud, prolonged cry. Startled, she dropped the rock and froze. It was sadness itself. But not a human cry, more like an animal.

Stop. Leave in peace, please, please …

Vanessa wrung her hands; she needed to look inside and yet she knew she shouldn't be doing this. Just like the pictures in the cupboard, she thought, as the image of herself surrounded by paintings of the

Loch Ness Monster sprang into her head. Nessie? What had she to do with this? She put her hand on another rock and waited for another warning cry, but nothing came, so she lifted another off the top and tried to peer inside. It was too dark. She would need a torch — but a glowing sock would do. Even dangling her sock over the opening, she could see nothing at first. Then her eye caught a glint of metal. Should she touch it? She waited for an image or a voice to guide her, but nothing came.

Carefully, so that she didn't disturb the stone pyramid, she put her hand inside. Her fingers touched something hard and she pulled her hand out again. Feeling less brave, she sat for a little while. She had to see what it was. Again she plunged her hand in and tried to peer in at the same time. Her fingers closed around what felt like a little chain and she lifted her hand out slowly.

At the end of the chain that dangled between her fingers was a locket. A tiny silver locket, old and badly tarnished. She fingered it gently and then opened it. Inside was a black and white photograph. It was clearly a woman, maybe in her thirties, but her features were hard to make out as part of the picture had lifted. Her hair was smooth and cut to her shoulders and Vanessa could see that she was very beautiful indeed. There was something about her face that made Vanessa feel sad. She sat down and leaned back against the wall to think.

Who was she and how had her picture got here, under a pile of rocks? Questions with no answers; more confusion. It was exhausting trying to sort it out. She needed to swim; she needed to be in the water to cool her brain.

Vanessa closed the locket and cleaned it as best she could on her jeans and then put it around her neck. Luckily, the chain was long enough to go over her head, as the clasp was rusted and couldn't be opened. Her dad would oil it for her. Dad. In her mind, she saw him for a second in the front seat of a car. She could see the back of his neck and the flecks of grey through his hair. He was driving; he was driving to … But her mind, playing tricks again, shut down. Tears pricked at the corner of her eyes in frustration. Why couldn't she remember? Why wouldn't this dream let her go?

Vanessa stood at the edge, cupping the locket tightly in her palm, and then, without even looking, she jumped out high into the air before plunging deep into the water below.

CHAPTER 22

On 27 July 1973, five people outside the Foyers Hotel watched something move quickly across the loch. One witness, Mr E. Moran from Yorkshire, said, 'although I was a sceptic before now, I don't mind what anyone else thinks – I am convinced that I have seen a creature of some kind in Loch Ness'.

Alan and Luke decided that they would go into the village with Lee to ask about Vanessa, while Maggie and Ronan stayed at the cottage in case she turned up. Alan tried hard to stay focused on the most likely possibilities and the relief he would feel when she sauntered up to him without even realising that she had caused such worry. He pleaded with Marie in his head, begged her to help him. He couldn't lose Vanessa too.

He pictured her face, her playful smile and tousled hair that gave her such a careless appearance and belied her sharp, inquisitive mind. He had to admit that this wasn't like Vanessa at all.

They talked to everyone in the village, from the lock keeper to Mrs MacNab and her daughters who worked in the grocery store, but there had been no sightings of Vanessa at all in the village that afternoon. Alan felt his heart begin to thump hard in his chest.

'What now? Luke's question was almost inaudible.

It was really dark now, and getting cold as they made their way back, running most of the way to the cottage in the hope of some news there. Alan slowed with a stitch in his side. He was either more unfit than he thought or panic was constricting every muscle in his body.

'Where's the closest police station, Lee?' Alan's voice was dull with pain.

'I'll call when we get back. It's Graham Maguire in Drumnadrochit we need. Maggie knows him well.'

'Luke and I will get some torches and walk along

the loch edge. Maybe she's fallen somewhere and twisted her ankle in the dark.' His voice grew stronger.

Luke looked at him with a hunted expression. His mouth was in a grim line and he was on the brink of tears.

'We're going to find her, Luke. I promise you.'

The road back to the cottage stretched before them interminably as they made their way home in silence, each deep in thought, each terrified at the possibilities. They scanned the ditches and hedgerows for any signs – half in dread, half in hope.

None of them saw the small figure run out onto the cottage driveway, but they began to sprint as soon as the shouting started. Someone was waving a torch and screaming up ahead.

'It's Ronan, Dad,' Luke shouted as he sped ahead of the other two. Within seconds, they were all standing in a bunch on the roadside, Alan on one knee, holding Ronan.

'Dad.' Ronan's breath heaved in his chest. 'Dad, the rowing boat's gone. Vanessa has taken the boat out. And she's on her own.'

CHAPTER 23

A model Nessie was made for the film The Private Life of Sherlock Holmes. *This model was towed around the loch by a submersible to see if it could lure the real Nessie into the open. After the model accidentally sank, it was never seen again.*

Vanessa felt more comfortable in the water now than out of it. Between eating the moss she took longer trips deep down into the water, where at last she met a school of fish that swam past her. Her eyes widened in astonishment. Something alive at last.

Arctic char, she shouted in her head. She remembered them from Maggie's description of the fish in the loch. Oh my God, the loch! Loch Ness, of course, and Maggie and her cottage. Her excitement at remembering a few snippets more of her life was intense. She turned around as quickly as she could and tried to swim after the school of char. To her surprise, she was able to keep up with the fish. They seemed entirely uninterested in her and so she swam on just behind them.

Swim down deep enough and you'll find me.

She swam on, although it was increasingly hard to go down, the physical pressure on her body growing with each stroke. Suddenly, she saw the fish turn and dart away.

She was aware now of a large shape glowing at a distance beyond her. Vanessa blinked, trying to make some sense of what she was looking at. A huge object moved slowly towards her.

Don't worry, I won't hurt you.

Vanessa stopped swimming, waiting for the inevitable. As it approached her, the glow grew more intense and the water warmer. She closed her eyes. Maybe she would wake from the dream any second now. But when she opened them again, she found herself face to face with large seal-like eyes, only a couple of inches away from her. She felt their intensity as they searched for something in her own eyes, something beyond her eyes, some connection with her, deep inside. A bubble of excitement seemed to burst inside Vanessa, and she was gripped by a sense of elation like she had never felt before.

The creature was exactly as in the painting, exactly like her dream. Vanessa stared straight into the eyes of the most wonderful cryptid in the world and a huge smile spread across her face. This was no dream. Her chest tightened again and this time Vanessa knew that it was only her ribs stopping her from bursting with happiness.

Put your arms around my neck and I'll show you my loch.

The voice in her head at last made sense to Vanessa. It had been Nessie all the time. She wrapped her arms around Nessie's slim neck, the warmth of her great body a pleasure and a comfort to her.

You're a mammal, you're warm-blooded. I knew it. Vanessa thought and smiled at Nessie.

Just like you, Nessie said simply.

Startled, Vanessa let go. She hadn't realised that the thought transfer worked both ways.

Better hold on tight.

And with that she moved off at speed, and Vanessa

could feel the rhythmic beating of Nessie's fins around her waist, and at her feet the second set of smaller flippers. Nessie was about 10 feet long and yet she moved effortlessly through the water.

It was like being on whaleback, speeding through the sea!

Yes, I remember the sea; at least I think I do. My mother – she's dead now – she used to talk about our home in the sea.

Dead. Dead. A wash of sadness swept through Vanessa, with such intensity that she felt her limbs go weak. Suddenly, she saw her own mother, small and frail, propped up in a bed with white pillows. Her dark hair was spread out like a fan behind her. Not the bouncy black hair that she used to have, but the limp and dull hair at the end.

The sadness was followed by a piercing pain in her chest as she watched the picture of her mother fade in her mind.

Hold me tight, Vanessa.

Vanessa did as Nessie said and, as they swam, she felt the pain ebb slowly away. The warmth of Nessie's body soothed her. They seemed to swim for an age in silence. The rhythm and the flow of the water over her body calmed Vanessa.

They must have gone quite deep before Vanessa noticed a shape looming ahead.

Look, Nessie. What's that?

Oh, that boat sank a long time ago. Want to see?

They swam alongside the boat and Vanessa looked in through the windows. It was a beautiful motorboat, long and elegant. The wood inside seemed to gleam as if it had just recently been polished. It was beautifully preserved.

There have been so many boats across my loch – parties; tourists; people looking for me, I think. There are huge eels, though, and people don't like that.

No, I wouldn't either, thought Vanessa as she looked around nervously.

Only a few have ever come down into my world, but there was a young woman on this boat; I tried to save her. I brought her back to the cave when I found her drowning, but it was no use.

Vanessa felt the huge creature's sadness.

How come I survived? she asked. I didn't drown.

I suppose it was because you believed in me and weren't afraid. Even though I told her – that other poor girl – to eat the green glow, she wouldn't. Maybe she couldn't hear me. She just went to sleep and never woke up.

Vanessa stroked the side of Nessie's neck with her hand. It felt so soft to her touch.

Those that drown are innocent and those that survive the douking are witches … The thought snaked through Vanessa's mind. Who had said it to her? She couldn't recall, yet a faint flicker of recognition made her feel uncomfortable.

Well, go on, finish your story, about the girl.

I brought her body back up as close to the surface as I dared. I couldn't risk being seen. Unfortunately, the divers who were looking for her saw me and they panicked. I have one of their cameras still in one of the caves if you want to see it?

She lifted her head and looked into Vanessa's eyes again.

You believe in me, Vanessa. I'll make everything all right for you, I promise. Now hold on, your glow is fading. I need to get you back to the caves.

Once they were back at the caves, Vanessa climbed out of the water and gathered some more moss to eat.

Tell me about your mother, she asked Nessie. How did she die?

She was sick for a long time. It all began when we came through the gates.

What kind of gates? asked Vanessa. Oh, you mean, lock-gates?

I don't remember. I was chasing some fish, I think, and I followed them through the first gate from the sea. My mother came after me but it was too late. We were forced to keep going through all the gates, and we ended up here, and she'd been hurt.

How? Did she get caught in the gates?

No, we swam under the boats, and when the water got shallow, in the canal, my mother was crushed.

Nessie stopped for a moment.

She never really recovered from that. Since she died, I've been on my own.

My mother died too, said Vanessa faintly.

But you have others don't you?

The thought echoed with clarity in Vanessa's mind, touching something familiar, something important that was hiding in her subconscious.

I heard you call Luke, Ronan and Alan. Who are they?

Vanessa closed her eyes in confusion. She tried hard to make sense of the mass of images that streamed through her head – Ronan laughing and throwing snowballs at her, Luke busy burying her legs in the sand on a beach. And her dad with his arms

130

outstretched as she ran towards him.

You're right; I do have others. I'm not alone. But what about you? Why don't you go back to the sea?

Go back? I couldn't do that. I'd get hurt, killed, just like my mother.

Vanessa began to eat the moss off the walls again. She was comfortable down here with Nessie.

My mother's bones are in the cave above, under the stones that I asked you not to touch.

Vanessa was taken aback.

How on earth did you get them up there?

Lena climbed up with them. She made … a grave, she called it.

Vanessa's mind raced. Lena. Lena … Where did she know that name from? She fingered the locket around her neck.

She had just lost her mother too, Nessie explained. *That's her mother's picture in the locket. After she'd buried the bones for me I helped her home.*

Vanessa felt her mind shutting down. It was too much to take in, bones, lockets, drownings …

You're tired, Vanessa. You should sleep.

CHAPTER 24

In the summer of 1969, the hunt for Nessie was intense. Scientists were using a submarine called Viperfish *and a small submersible called* Pieces *to dive down deep into the loch. They went to 820 feet which was actually deeper than the loch's official maximum depth. At 750 feet they found strange, whirlpool currents and elsewhere the crew noticed fish and eels with 'unusual colourings'.*

The old green rowing boat was too leaky to take out on the loch, so Lee had called Frank Dobson to bring around his speedboat. Maggie's kitchen was full of people, not loud or boisterous this time, but subdued and silent. Constable Graham Maguire from

Drumnadrochit had been called and was on his way from Inverness where he had been attending a police conference. He promised he would be there within the hour.

The roar of the speedboat echoed through the kitchen door and brought them all into the garden. Three boats instead of one. The two speedboats came to a sudden halt at the mooring and behind them, at a slow and determined pace, a fishing boat with an outboard engine struggled to keep up.

'That's Frank's son, Hamish, with the outboard and John Nolan, another neighbour in the other speedboat,' Maggie explained to Alan, as they hurried down the garden to meet them.

'They have powerful lights on board those speedboats. It's the only way we'll find the rowing boat at this time of night. We will find it, Alan.' Maggie pressed her hand firmly on his forearm as she said it.

Alan was past caring about platitudes and terrified that they would find the boat but not Vanessa. He felt a rush of irritation with Maggie. None of them could know what this torture was like for him. Losing Vanessa would be unbearable. He had to find her.

CHAPTER 25

In the 1930s, there was a reward of £20,000 offered for the live capture of the Loch Ness Monster.

Vanessa climbed back up to the pile of stones that guarded the bones of Nessie's mother. She was curious about it. Maybe she could find more clues about that girl, Lena, whoever she was.

She found the climb harder this time than before. She paused for a moment and looked down, but there was no sign of Nessie. She stared at the water, feeling its draw but also needing to reach the cave.

Once inside the cave again, she sat beside the pile of rocks where Lena had made a kind of grave for the bones. Lena — of course! That was the name of the girl she'd read about in one of those cuttings she'd found. She'd gone missing, hadn't she?

Vanessa took a stone from the pile and waited for Nessie to talk to her, but nothing happened, so she removed a few more. She dismantled the pyramid stone by stone until she saw the first bone. It was a curved rib bone, she guessed, at least 3 feet long. She ran her fingers along the smooth edge and tried to visualise the size of Nessie's mother. She must have been huge when she came into the loch. Nessie was clearly not yet fully grown. If she was to travel back to the sea, now was the time to do it, while she was still small enough not to get crushed by boats in the shallow parts of the canal. Yes! She had to find Nessie. She had to persuade her to try.

She placed the bones carefully back in their grave and piled the rocks back up. Still no communication from Nessie. How could she help her home? She sat back against the cave wall and closed her eyes to imagine it. She could draw a map. She knew the way, and she could explain it all to Nessie.

She climbed down quickly to the lower cave to look for Nessie. No sign.

Picking up a sharp piece of stone, Vanessa began to

draw on the softer surface of the cave wall. She drew a route map for Nessie, a picture of the journey from Loch Ness through the canal and the series of lock-gates she'd need to negotiate to get back to the sea.

The first lock-gate is Lock Dochgarroch. There are four more at Muirtown. Then you're at the sea-locks at Inverness. Once you're through those, you swim under the enormous bridge, Kessock Bridge it's called, and out to sea, the Atlantic Ocean. It's as easy as that, Nessie, and remember, you're still quite small, you won't get hurt.

But Nessie didn't answer.

Finally, Vanessa put a large arrow, pointing in the right direction. Thank God she had studied the maps of the Caledonian Canal and the lock-gates as well as she had.

If Nessie wasn't going to talk to her, she'd better go and find her. Quickly scraping another handful of moss from the cave wall, she dived in.

She swam down and down. Nothing. Where was Nessie?

She was starting to feel cold now. She'd never felt cold before, no matter how deep she'd swum down. And it was getting darker. Was her glow starting to fade? She could barely see her own hands and arms through the murky water.

Her chest tightened and she felt herself sinking.

Look at the map, Nessie, she thought urgently as the blackness engulfed her. It'll show you the way.

CHAPTER 26

On 15 October 2005, Robbie Girvan, owner of the Loch Ness Caravan Park at Invermoriston was out at 6pm walking his dogs on the loch shore. He saw a creature, which he described as having a 4 foot high head and neck, rise out of the water. Previously a non-believer, he said that the 'dark green and silvery' creature could only have been Nessie.

It took less than five minutes for the lights of the powerboat to pick out the upturned rowing boat. Alan's heart sank. Why was it overturned? He felt as if he might get sick over the side of the boat any minute. Frank used his walkie-talkie to call in his son.

'Hamish, we've found the boat. We're about 200 metres east of Morag's place. We'll need all the light we can get.'

But Alan couldn't wait. Within seconds, he had taken off his boots and coat and dived into the cold water. There was no way Vanessa could have survived long in these icy temperatures. With each strong stroke, he said her name in his head until he reached the rowing boat. It was pitch black when he went under it, and he flailed his arms about, his hands banging off the wood, in the desperate hope of finding her. When he came back up, they were all waiting in silence. He shook his head weakly and heard a cry which he guessed was either Ronan or Luke.

Frank leaned over and yanked him, dripping, onto the floor of the motorboat. Lee stumbled over to him.

'OK, Hamish,' Frank was shouting into the radio, 'we've found the boat upturned, but no sign of Vanessa yet. Let's start scanning the water with the lights. But let's be organised about it. You take from Morag's in about 100 metres, I'll take the next 100, and John will head out a bit farther. She must be somewhere close by.'

He turned to Alan, who was still crouched on the floor of the boat.

'The police have arrived at Maggie's and are getting another couple of boats to –'

Cutting across Frank came a loud and terrifying screech, not from a human but a bird. A large black hawk circled the boat and then swooped down aggressively. It was so close that Lee thought she felt the tip of a wing flap against the top of her head. She covered her head with her arms, shaking in disbelief. Looking up through her crossed arms, she saw him wheel in the air, turning back to make a second swoop. And at that moment, as clearly as if she was floating out of her body and looking down through the hawks' eyes, she saw herself lying on the bank over near Bell's Point. This had happened before; she had been a child, maybe nine or ten at the time.

'She's on the bank, at Bell's Point, I know it.'

Everybody stared at Lee, unclear how to react. Had she lost it, or did she really know something? Either way, she was acting strangely. Everyone waited for Alan to say something. He looked at Lee and, seeing the terror in her face, shouted to Frank.

'OK, get us into the bank at Bell's Point. Lee, you go to the bow and see if you can see the spot where you think she is.'

Although he didn't mean it, he seemed to say the

word think with more emphasis that he had intended. But Lee didn't appear to notice, she just scrambled up to the bow and then quite inexplicably shouted back to Frank.

'The hawk; just follow the hawk in to the bank.'

Frank shook his head in disbelief, but revved the boat a little and headed towards the bank. He didn't want to cut through the water too quickly in case they missed Vanessa or, worse, hit her in the water. He made steady progress towards the bank but it felt like a lifetime for Alan. His eyes almost hurt as he glared ahead, trying to see farther into the dark than the light allowed him.

'Look,' Lee screamed. 'Look, she's there!'

Alan scanned the bank where Lee was looking. It was still too dark to make out anything other than outline shapes.

'See there!' Lee pointed and shouted, almost hysterical now. As Alan peered ahead, he saw the rock-shaped mound near the water's edge turn into the body of his daughter.

'Hurry, Frank. She's there. She's there.'

As he drew closer, Alan all but knocked Lee into the water, as he pushed passed her at the bow and jumped at least 6 feet from the edge of the boat on to the bank.

CHAPTER 27

In 1975, Bob Rines, an American scientist, captured some extraordinary pictures using a motor driven camera and strobe light at a depth of about 45 feet. The best showed Nessie's long, outstretched neck and front body complete with flippers and was published that year in the top scientific journal, Nature.

Alan held Vanessa tightly in his arms as he climbed back into the boat, crushing her to his breast bone as if he would never let her go. Luke pressed forward, but her father enveloped her protectively. She seemed OK, apart from the large bruise on her forehead, and her breathing and pulse were even. Luke stood beside him and stroked Vanessa's hair. Where was Ronan? Alan looked round and saw that he was sitting on the floor of the boat, clutching his knees, while tears streamed unchecked down his face.

'She'll be fine, love, I promise,' Alan said to him in a whisper. 'She must have managed to swim ashore and then conked out.'

Alan looked with such intensity at his daughter's beautiful face that he thought he might collapse any moment. He couldn't understand it. She wasn't wearing socks or shoes. Why was she not frozen stiff? He shook the thoughts from his head. He had her in his arms, she was alive, and all he had to do was get her to a doctor.

'Where's the closest hospital?' he shouted to Frank over the noise of the engine, as they started back to the cottage.

'Inverness,' Frank answered promptly. 'It will take at least an hour in the car.'

'No. Call Maggie and tell her to get Doc Morris.' Lee's voice was small and faint, but she said it with such certainty that Alan just nodded his agreement to Frank. She didn't look at Alan; she seemed to be lost in her own world.

Into the silence, Lee repeated herself.

'Tell Maggie to get Doc Morris. He'll know.'

Alan just nodded again to Frank and then looked back down at Vanessa's mop of dark hair. 'I love you, my angel,' he whispered, 'and I'm so sorry, I'm so sorry.'

The whole village seemed to be at the bottom of the garden to meet them. Alan kept his head down, not wanting to catch anybody's eye, as he got off the boat. He just had to get Vanessa inside safely. As he walked up the garden, carrying her still in his arms, he saw the headlights of a car pulling into the driveway.

'It's Doc Morris,' Maggie said as she walked beside him. 'You take her up straight to her bed and I'll send him to you.'

When Alan returned to the kitchen, a silence fell. Constable Maguire was still there, sitting at the table over a large mug of coffee. The boys, Lee and Maggie were sitting in various positions around the room. Maggie must have sent the rest home, thank God.

Alan chose his words carefully.

'She's going to be OK. She opened her eyes for a few moments, although it was a pretty glazed look and I'm not sure she recognised me. Then she faded out again. Dr Morris says she'll come around in her own time. She's just exhausted by the whole experience.'

Now he looked across at his two sons.

'Guys, you should get some rest too. You're wiped out. Go on, up you go.'

He hugged them both and then watched them go without a murmur of protest. Thank God they were sharing a room, he thought, Ronan would certainly need Luke tonight. Their shoulders were hunched and they looked older than their years. Not a night easily forgotten.

Alan sighed and slumped into the nearest chair.

CHAPTER 28

In 1952, Dr Richard Synge, an eminent scientist and winner of the Nobel Prize for Chemistry in 1938, was staying at Fort Augustus with his parents and sisters. They witnessed a 'dark, hump-like object in the loch' close to the bank which was moving quickly and left a slight wake. They followed it by car for about 3 miles. After that the creature 'became stationary and then submerged'.

The tension in the room was terrible. Despite his relief at finding Vanessa unhurt, Alan knew that there was something still amiss. He looked across at Lee, who was distracted and distant. Her hands were wrapped around a large mug but she never once raised it to her lips. He glanced across at Maggie to find that she was watching Lee also. To his surprise, she caught his eye and made an almost imperceptible shake of her head. What the hell was going on?

'Lee, my love ...' Maggie hesitated and waited for Lee to lift her head and look at her. 'Why don't you get yourself upstairs too? You need a good night's rest.'

Lee stood slowly and moved to the door. Before she went out, she turned and said to nobody in particular, 'I have to talk to her.'

'Not tonight, Lee. Better in the morning when she's recovered.'

Alan looked bemused. He turned to look at Lee and then back to Maggie, trying to pick up some clue as to what was going on. They gave nothing away; Maggie's face was closed tight, devoid of any expression and Lee's so drained that he thought she might collapse any moment. Finally, Lee agreed to go to bed, but refused Maggie's help getting there.

'I'd prefer to be on my own.'

There was a long silence after she left. The strain of it was getting unbearable when Maggie spoke.

'Coffee, Alan?'

He winced as he took a drink from the large mug. It was milky and poisonously sweet.

'You're soaked to the skin, Alan. There's plenty of hot water for a bath.'

Alan sat in silence waiting for an explanation of Lee's behaviour. He was not ready to ask directly but not willing to ignore it either.

'I'll have a bath after the doctor is gone and after I've checked on Vanessa again.'

Another silence ensued. It was Constable Maguire who broke it this time.

'It's happened before,' he said, looking directly at Alan, his forehead creased in worry.

'What?' Alan jerked upright in his chair as if he had been jabbed with a knife.

'It's happened before, but for longer,' he repeated in a monotone. He turned to Maggie. 'Tell him, Maggie. He needs to know.'

Alan jumped out of his seat, electrified with terror. Vanessa had been abducted by some local nut who had taken other kids before and they were only telling him now? His anger surfacing, he said grimly through gritted teeth, 'I think one of you better tell me quickly.'

Maggie stood up and opened the drawer of the

Welsh dresser. She pulled out a pile of papers and leafed through them. Finally, she went over to Alan and put a newspaper cutting in his hand. He saw that it was aged and yellowing. He read the date: 7 May 1986.

Local Girl Missing.

Lena Cook, a twelve-year-old from Fort Augustus went missing yesterday morning. She was last seen by her family outside her home near the Loch edge. As she had only recently moved to the region she was not familiar with the area and her family are concerned that she may have had an accident. Searches are continuing and police are anxious for any information at all. Please contact Constable Maguire at Drumnadrochit police station.

There was a small black-and-white photo of a girl's face. She looked young and ill at ease.

Alan looked up, puzzled.

'What has this to do with Vanessa?'

'That was Lee.'

'Lee? It says Lena Cook.' Alan was still no clearer.

'Lee is short for Lena. And Cook was her surname when she came from America after her parents died.

McDonald was her mother's maiden name and is mine. She must have felt a need to fit in to this small community ...' Maggie caught the fleeting look of irritation on Alan's face and hurried on. 'So she insisted on changing it to McDonald when she was about twelve. Not long after it happened, really.'

'So what did happen to her?' Alan demanded, intent on trying to clear up the confusion that he felt. 'Where did she go and how does it have anything to do with what happened to Vanessa?

Nobody offered an explanation, but a picture of Lee's shocked face on the boat yelling about Bell's Point rose in front of him.

Maguire finally answered him.

'We don't know. She was found like Vanessa on the bank, wet but not cold, unconscious but unharmed.'

'But surely she told you what happened, Maggie?'

'No, not really. She wouldn't talk about it at first and would only say that she hadn't been frightened and that nobody had hurt her. In fact, she later claimed she wasn't with anyone else, that she had an adventure like Alice in Wonderland and had fallen asleep on the bank. All I know is that it has something to do with the magic of the loch.'

Alan stared at Maggie in disbelief. The magic of the loch! Had Maggie lost the plot entirely?

'Where had she been?' Alan insisted loudly, deeply frustrated by the conversation.

'In Loch Ness,' Maggie answered calmly.

'Well, I know that. You said she was wet.'

'Alan, we searched every inch of the bank that day and the next and she wasn't there. But that was where we found her in the end, on the bank at Bell's Point, exactly where you found Vanessa.'

'But …' Alan stopped and looked at Maggie.

'We had lots of questions too, Alan, but we never really got many answers, so we came to accept it in the end. She didn't seem to remember much of what had happened. And from that time on, Lee settled where she had been restless before. She made friends and learned to love it here after a very rocky start. But above all, she started to accept her mother's death.'

'I thought her mother and father died in the same accident?' Alan said.

'Aye, so they did. But her father was a more distant figure to her. He had travelled with his job most of her young life, so it was her mother's death she took hardest.'

Alan felt in a state of surreal exhaustion. He had

no idea what was going on. He looked up when Dr Morris opened the door to the kitchen and stuck his head around it.

'Not interrupting, am I? Just thought I'd let you know that she's fine. A sturdy wee lass, I can tell.'

He had a cheerful, professional face and the sight of it made Alan's heart lurch. There had been so many composed, good-natured doctors' faces in the years of Marie's illness and even at the end, not one had prepared him adequately for her death.

'Yes, but did you examine her?' Alan almost shouted.

The doctor, undisturbed by Alan's manner, answered mildly. 'Aye, a wee bruise on her forehead, but apart from that she's fine, just exhausted really. I've never seen such white skin, it's almost as if it's see-through. But she's good and healthy, and she'll get back her colour in no time. She's in a deep sleep now, but will need one of your hearty breakfasts tomorrow, Maggie.'

Alan didn't have time to listen to any more chat. He took the stairs two at a time.

He opened the door of Vanessa's room, carefully, so as not to make any noise. A small bedside lamp glowed softly beside her. She did look pale, a strange colour, but he was distracted by how young and peaceful she looked and tears gathered at the corners of his eyes. He held her wrist gently to feel the pulse for himself. It was as strong as his own. Kneeling down beside her, he brushed her mop of damp black curls off her face and pressed his lips to her forehead tenderly. He turned off the lamp and closed the door quietly. They would talk in the morning.

It was dark in the room. Dark except for the glow. Nobody was there to see the fading green luminescence of Vanessa's skin on the snow white sheets.

CHAPTER 29

On 28 September 1966, Count Emmanuel de Lichtervelde from Belgium and his driver, former naval officer Mr Guy Senior, saw a large, dark object with two distinct humps moving in the loch. Mr Senior believed that it was an animal rather than a moving boat. The count is reported to have said that it was the most wonderful thing that could ever have happened to him.

The next morning, Vanessa woke early. Her eyes fell on the small green table at the window. Window? What had happened? She wasn't in the water; she wasn't in the cave. How come she was back in her bedroom? And Nessie? Where was she?

She jumped out of bed and ran to the window, scanning the loch. Was Nessie still down there? Had she seen the map? Would she be able to read it?

Vanessa let her mind wander back. She remembered swimming in the deep with Nessie. She smiled at the thought of the mounds of moss she had eaten. It should make eating spinach easier now for sure.

A light knock on the door interrupted her thoughts. Vanessa froze. Should she make a dash for her bed and pretend to be still asleep? She wasn't sure if she could face everyone yet. How could she explain where she had been?

Lee put her head around the door cautiously. She was carrying a cup and she looked extremely pale, Vanessa thought.

'Come in, Lee.'

Lee crossed over to the window without catching Vanessa's eye and they both sat down in silence. She looked younger and frailer than before.

'Hot chocolate. I was pretty sure you could not face one of Maggie's breakfasts, this morning of all mornings.'

Vanessa smiled, but Lee didn't smile back. She was staring at Vanessa's neck intensely and the look of shock on her face was frightening. Instinctively, Vanessa put her hand up to her throat and then beneath her fingers she felt the locket and chain. Her heart skipped a beat. So it was true! She had been in Loch Ness.

'It's yours?' she asked in surprise, her voice a whisper. Lena. Lee.

Lee gave the tiniest of nods. Tears filled her eyes. Vanessa stared hard at her unsure what to say or do. She watched as Lee's tears spilled over and ran down the side of her nose. Lee made no effort to brush them away.

'My mother's,' she whispered. 'Where did you find it?'

'Don't you remember?' Vanessa replied, horrified at the thought of having to explain the cave and the grave. Lee must be the girl who had buried the bones.

'No. At least I don't think I do.' Lee hesitated. 'I lost it when I was about twelve, a year after my mother died.'

'But where did you lose it?' Vanessa demanded.

Lee eyed Vanessa warily.

'In the loch.'

'Good, 'cause that's where I found it.' Vanessa pulled it up over her head carefully and put it into

Lee's palm. Her hand looked tiny, as frail as a child's, Vanessa thought. She watched as Lee opened the oval locket. The most beautiful smile transformed her face through her tears. Pity rose in Vanessa's throat and she threw her arms around Lee's slight frame and held her as tightly as her childish arms could manage. Eventually, Lee pulled back.

'Where were you? Where did you go?' she asked eventually.

'You don't know?' Vanessa said.

Lee didn't bother to answer she just stared at the faded picture of her mother.

Vanessa stood up, walked across the room and opened the cupboard with the paints and canvases. Picking up one of the paintings she turned it around to Lee. It was a picture of Nessie swimming, exactly as Vanessa remembered her. 'You painted these?' Vanessa asked.

'Yes. They were dreams I had.'

Vanessa pulled out another where Nessie was glowing and in the background were outlines of some caves. Light green patches glowed on the walls.

'Some were weirder than others,' Lee made a half attempt at smiling.

'They weren't dreams,' Vanessa said hotly, annoyed

at Lee. 'You went missing didn't you? For days, just like me.'

'Days? Vanessa, you were only missing for hours. As far as we know, you went out in the boat in the afternoon and we found you at about eleven o'clock.'

Now it was Vanessa's turn to look puzzled.

'Not even a full day? she said faintly 'Are you sure?'

Lee nodded.

'Well, what happened to you then? The paper said you were missing for days. You are Lena Cook, aren't you?'

'Yes. I was. McDonald now. I prefer that.'

'I can't remember what happened that day. It's too long ago. I was concussed. I can't remember what happened.' She said it slower this time. 'Except that I fell into Loch Ness.'

'Yes, douked, just like me, and we both survived!' Vanessa smiled triumphantly. Her voice rose with excitement. 'We're both witches! Do you remember what Pat Mackay said about douking? Remember, those who survive are witches and are burned at the stake? She went on, tripping over her words. 'Think about it. You met Nessie and you swam with her and you buried her mother's bones in a pile of stones in a cave. You must remember.' She was sounding hysterical now she knew, but she had to make Lee remember. Vanessa grabbed Lee's hands roughly and squeezed them tight. 'Where did you put your mother's locket?'

Lee gasped and jerked her hands away from Vanessa's hold.

'How could you know that? That was my dream.' She sounded hurt.

'It wasn't a dream. That's what I'm telling you.'

Lee's tears had stopped with the turn in the conversation. Now she put her head between her hands to keep out Vanessa's words.

'Who found me? It was you, wasn't it?' Vanessa demanded. 'How?'

'They found me on the bank, at Bell's Point, just like you,' Lee said faintly. 'I put Mom's locket in the grave with the bones. I was angry with her for dying. And then when I came home, I felt so guilty for leaving it. It became easier as the memories faded, I suppose, to believe that it was all a dream. Well, who would believe it anyway? I don't believe it myself, even now.'

'I do,' Vanessa said quietly.

Lee took her hand and held it.

'Thanks for bringing it back to me.'

They sat without talking, each lost in their own thoughts.

'You did all those things too? The green moss stuff and swimming without breathing?'

Vanessa smiled. 'Wasn't it wonderful?'

'All these years, I've convinced myself that it was a dream but if you did it all too … '

'And it changed your life,' Vanessa said.

'Yes, meeting Nessie changed everything.'

'Me too.' Vanessa smiled at the woman she once hated.

She suddenly remembered drawing the map for Nessie. Had she found it? Had she understood it? Had she got home too?

She started to say something about it all to Lee, but Lee had stood up. There was a determined look on her face as she made a beeline for the cupboard. After much rummaging, she produced a battered looking copybook. She put it on the table between them. There was spindly writing in blue pen on the front, 'Lena Cook's Diary 1986'.

Vanessa opened the first page while Lee stared out of the window:

I don't want to forget a second of it. Maggie told me that I was gone for forty-eight hours, but it felt like weeks to me. She didn't let the policeman ask me questions, thank goodness. She says tomorrow will do, when I've slept, but it will be a different story by tomorrow. The true story will be locked away for good when I finish writing this.

I'm sitting by my window which looks over the loch. After every sentence, I stop and look for her. A ripple on the water makes my heart jump, but I haven't seen her. I can hardly breathe for missing her.

I must write it down even if no one believes me. I can see it all if I close my eyes: the colours, her smooth skin, her face. I can see the moss under my nails as I scrape it off the cave walls. I feel it soft and wet as it balls in my mouth and coats my tongue. It tingles. My skin begins to change. It turns a weird green at first and the more I eat, the more it glows. The water is different too. It should be cold and muddy, but it's not. It's so soft on my skin. I feel safe and happy. I know I should have drowned, but she saved me.

She let me talk about my parents, she knew exactly how it felt. People often say that 'life goes on', but it didn't for me. For me, it stopped in its tracks. It didn't teeter and fall, or wobble and slow, it just stopped dead. The days went on, sure, but not my life. How did I get from California to Inverness? I must have come by plane, Maggie must have met me, but I don't remember. I don't know what happened in the months after Mom and Dad died, but I can

161

remember the phone call when I heard the news. Even now, I remember picking up the phone in the hall. It was like a dead weight in my hand and I felt the hard plastic jammed into my ear.

'Sorry, I don't understand.'

The echo on the line didn't help. Perhaps the echo was in my head.

'Accident ... Both missing ... Rescue teams ... Not looking good ...'

He tried to say it kindly. I hate telephones.

I've never written about that day before. What was there to write about? Nothingness? Nobody could explain what happened to them. Now I can't explain what has happened to me. Perhaps I am mad. Perhaps I am a witch and I make these things happen. I don't know. But what I do know is that she saved my life. She gave it back to me and now I've got a second chance.

Vanessa closed the copybook.

'Wow, you could really write when you were young. Maybe you should write our story some day.'

'You missed a bit,' Lee said. 'Look at the last page.'

Vanessa opened it to the last page.

Perhaps monsters like Nessie are too strange to be true or maybe people can only describe what they know and what they've seen before.

I read a story once about explorers in Australia hundreds of years ago who wrote about creatures that had heads like deer, stood upright like men and leapt like frogs. Sometimes, they even had two heads, one on top and another on the stomach. Monsters to them, but we know now that these monsters are just kangaroos. Maybe in the future, we'll be talking about Nessie in the same way.

CHAPTER 30

The idea of a Loch Ness monster may indeed sound strange. But is it any stranger than other animals we have only recently discovered? The colossal squid is even larger than the giant squid. It was first identified from remnants in the stomach of a sperm whale in 1925 and the first mature specimen was only found in 2007. Or the coelacanth, a living fossil thought to be extinct for 65 million years, which was rediscovered by scientists in 1938.

The next two hours were something that Lee could never have imagined happening. They both took turns to tell each other their stories. Lee had heard a little of Marie's illness and death from Alan, but told with the honesty of a child, she felt the raw pain of the whole family. Then Lee told Vanessa all about her childhood and her parents' death, or at least what little she knew. Poor Lee. Her parents' bodies had never been recovered, and she still didn't know the details of their accident thirty-four years later.

In the months after their disappearance, she had been sent away from everything she knew in America to a strange country. Alone. An only child. Worst of all, she had no irritating brothers to help her forget. No one to share her unhappiness or to share new happiness when it eventually came.

'Of course, I had Maggie,' Lee said lovingly. 'And it was her strength that got me through.'

'With a bit of help from Nessie of course,' Vanessa said with a grin.

When they had exhausted themselves talking and Vanessa felt she could face the family, the two of them went downstairs side by side. Alan looked up from the table as they came in. They stood close to each other, their arms touching. He had been thinking through all the questions he would ask Vanessa, but now the relief at seeing them both look so happy made him stop and think again. Maggie had suggested leaving them to 'work things out', but he hadn't imagined that they would talk for hours, or that they would actually end up friends. At least that was the way it looked from where he was sitting. What exactly were they working out anyway? Would he ever get an explanation for yesterday? He was beginning to doubt it.

'You want an omelette, Vanessa? Maggie has just taught me how to cook one.'

Alan wondered if Ronan would even mention her near drowning or would he just take up from where they had left off.

'Thanks, Ronan. I'm starving. I could eat a horse, but an omelette will have to do.' Vanessa went over to look at the pan.

'That's it?' she said in a disgusted voice.

God, things were certainly back to normal. Alan sighed.

Lee sat down at the table beside him and kissed him lightly on the cheek.

'She's fine,' she murmured in his ear.

'Only joking, Ronan. It looks great, really. I love lots of cheese.' Vanessa made a semi-gracious effort to backtrack.

'Perhaps.' Alan smiled back at Lee.

It was Luke who brought it up.

'So what happened, Vanessa?' Luke asked abruptly. All eyes turned on Vanessa, including Lee's, and they waited.

'Well,' she paused. She had rehearsed this part. 'I decided to take the boat out just a tiny distance from the bank. I'm really not the appalling rower that you think I am, Luke.' She stopped, her flow halted by his scathing look.

'I'm not sure you can say that after nearly drowning, Vanessa.' Luke was not letting her off that easily. She had given them all a serious scare.

'OK, I know I shouldn't have, sorry.' She sounded apologetic this time. 'Then the wind blew up and my oar slipped out of the oarlock. When I tried to get it back I fell over the edge and I must have hit my head.'

'But how did you get to the bank?' Luke persisted.

'I don't know, really. I suppose that before I blacked out, I must have swum back to the bank. I don't remember, though. I suppose I was concussed.'

Alan kept his mouth firmly shut.

'But why did you take the boat out on your own in the first place?' Luke demanded.

'Well, Dad did say that we would go out on the

loch at half past four. So I was just doing what he said.'

'Oh, Vanessa, don't!' her father pleaded. 'I can't bear to think what could have happened to you.' His eyes filled with tears.

She ran around the table and flung her arms around him.

'Dad, I'm so sorry. I didn't mean it. I'm sorry for everything.' This time she really meant it. It must have been awful for them all.

He buried his face in her hair and hugged her back violently.

'Excuse me, Vanessa.' Ronan stood patiently with the frying pan, scooping a mess of eggs onto a plate beside her. 'Are you going to eat this omelette or will I pass it on to someone more deserving?'

Vanessa gave her dad a light kiss on the top of his head as she stood up.

'Is there any ketchup, Ronan? I'm sure it will taste great, but a smothering of red sauce might help to take the look off it.' She grinned wickedly at her brother.

Ronan went to the fridge and pulled out a bottle of ketchup. He shook it hard as he walked over to Vanessa, opened it and then squeezed the plastic bottle with all his might. There was a cartoon-sounding splat as the ketchup hit her blue T-shirt full on and then, with the help of gravity, glooped down on to her left shoe.

Luke snorted, spraying his cup of tea across the table. He coughed and laughed at the same time.

'You know, I've wanted to do something like that for months now,' Ronan said, his eyes dancing with mischief as he watched Vanessa to see how she would react.

Vanessa was stunned. She stood immobile, except for her fingers rubbing the stain on her shirt. There was a long pause before her head slumped forward, her shoulders began to shake and she abandoned herself to a fit of giggles, the like of which they had not heard in years.

CHAPTER 31

The famous author G.K. Chesterton said that 'many a man has been hanged on less evidence than there is for the Loch Ness Monster'.

On their final day in the cottage, nobody talked much and there was a strange feeling of anticipation in the air. Everything was packed and yet there was not enough time to do anything or go anywhere. Vanessa moved sluggishly around the kitchen, her head filled with thoughts of Nessie and her journey home. She had spent much of the morning sitting at the window twisting her mother's engagement ring that she still wore on her middle finger, while her eyes scanned the loch for Nessie. Part of Vanessa wanted just one last glimpse of her but the other part hoped that she was no longer there, that she had made it back to the sea.

She poured a glass of orange juice and sat in front of it while her fingers curled and uncurled the edge of the morning newspaper.

'Sad to be going?'

She looked up as Luke threw himself into the chair opposite her, his hair tousled and his eyes half shut with sleep. Luke liked his sleep.

'I suppose so. It has felt so long though. It's hard to believe it was only a few days.'

'Yeah. It felt like a lifetime to me.' His voice was grim.

Vanessa's eyes filled quickly with tears and she drank her glass of orange juice, as if she was suddenly parched, to cover them up. She had given them all a scare and, for that, she felt bad. But she had also had the most amazing experience of her life. She had swum and talked with Nessie. Nessie – a cryptid that others had hunted for hundreds of years and she had found her. Well, she and Lee, really.

Finally, the moment came to leave. In the noise and bustle of their last goodbyes, rounds of hugs and kisses and promises to return, Vanessa found herself standing awkwardly beside Lee. It was as if they had shared too much too quickly and she felt almost embarrassed by their intimacy. Vanessa could also see her father's surprise at their sudden friendship and as she had no intention of sharing their secret any time soon, she reverted to her old ways – Vanessa ignored Lee.

They piled into the car, her brothers in the back seat, her father driving. She was in the front seat this time – not as a map reader, but so that her father could keep an eye on her, Vanessa imagined. He had barely left her side since she had been found.

Looking out at the sunlight glinting off the loch and Maggie and Lee standing under the arch of flowers at the front door was almost too much for Vanessa. Maggie was waving cheerfully, but Lee's hands hung at her sides. As her father started the engine, Vanessa flung open the car door and made a dash for them. Hugging Maggie first, she squeezed Lee even harder and was delighted to feel her kiss the top of her head.

'See you in Dublin?' Vanessa asked Lee, hopefully.

'Try and keep me away,' she replied, laughing.

Every few minutes, Vanessa craned her neck for

her last look at Loch Ness as the dark waters disappeared and reappeared through the trees that lined the shores of the loch. She had an ache in her heart at leaving and yet she was excited at the thought of getting home and going back up to the attic. There were loads more cryptid files up there and she was the only person in the world who knew about them. She slipped her hand into her pocket and fingered the wrinkly surface of her shrunken head. It already felt like her oldest friend. Could it really have only been a few weeks since she found it? Turning on the radio in an attempt to distract herself she moved through the channels until she heard the excited voice of a young reporter.

Reports of sightings have flooded in all morning. It seems that Inverness has its own monster. She's already been christened 'Invernessie.' First to report the sighting were a group of twenty three children on a school bus. At eight thirty this morning, on their way to school, they witnessed a monster, which was as long as the bus, in the Beauly Firth. It had an eel-like neck, a large hump, and moved slowly in the water. The sighting took place not far from the Clachnaharry sea lock at the northern end of the Caledonian Canal. They watched the creature for at least five minutes as it headed seaward before it dived beneath the surface and disappeared without a trace. Further sightings were reported throughout the day. Unfortunately, not a single person who saw 'Invernessie' managed to get a photo of the monster.